A TIME FOR MURDER

Carlos Galecci, a top man in organized crime, has been murdered — and the manner of his death is extraordinary . . . He'd last been seen the previous night, entering his private vault, to which only he knew the combination. When he fails to emerge by the next morning, his staff have the metal door cut open — to discover Galecci dead with a knife in his back. Private detective Johnny Merak is hired to find the murderer and discover how the impossible crime was committed — but is soon under threat of death himself . . .

*Books by John Glasby
in the Linford Mystery Library:*

THE SAVAGE CITY

JOHN GLASBY

A TIME FOR MURDER

Complete and Unabridged

LINFORD
Leicester

First published in Great Britain

First Linford Edition
published 2007

British Library CIP Data

Glasby, John S. (John Stephen)
  A time for murder.—Large print ed.—
  Linford mystery library
  1. Private investigators—Fiction
  2. Murder—Investigation—Fiction
  3. Mafia—Fiction
  4. Detective and mystery stories
  5. Large type books
  I. Title
  823.9′14 [F]

  ISBN 978–1–84617–678–4

Published by
F. A. Thorpe (Publishing)
Anstey, Leicestershire

Set by Words & Graphics Ltd.
Anstey, Leicestershire
Printed and bound in Great Britain by
T. J. International Ltd., Padstow, Cornwall

This book is printed on acid-free paper

1

It was a little after six in the morning when I turned off the freeway and swung the old Merc towards downtown LA. A misty November morning with a thin drizzle smearing the windscreen, making it difficult to see clearly.

The telephone call that had woken me nearly an hour earlier had come from Sam Rizzio, Carlos Galecci's right-hand man and I knew better than to ignore it.

I'd met Galecci for the first time three days before in a little Italian restaurant well off the main thoroughfares with two of his bruisers sitting a couple of tables away. They'd made themselves as inconspicuous as possible but they still stood out like sore thumbs.

Galecci was still one of the top men in the Organization if you believed everything you read in the papers. But to look at him you'd scarcely credit it. Short, going to fat in middle age, he looked mister average nice guy until you looked into his eyes. Cold and hard like those of a snake, they drilled right through you.

The conversation, which had lasted no more than fifteen minutes, was mainly one-sided. He did the talking and I did the listening. The gist of it was that he believed somebody was out to kill him and he wanted me to dig into things and find out who it was.

I knew that with his money and connections he could have hired the best private eye in town, maybe the best in the state. The fact that I'd been a small-time hood myself until I'd got a lucky break and went straight, didn't seem to bother him in the least. In fact, it seemed to make him more determined to hire me.

When he'd offered a thousand dollar retainer plus generous expenses, I'd figured — what the hell? At that rate I'd take the Devil's money so long as it didn't land me in jail again. After all, I had my license to think of.

Now this unexpected phone call and here I was, driving up to Galecci's place at this ungodly hour of the morning and wondering what I'd let myself in for.

I'd never been in this part of town before but it looked just like hundreds of others I'd known all my life. Sleazy bars, nightclubs and girlie shows; all blue, red and yellow strip lights still showing through the mist and rain. Shadows moving silently along the sidewalks; the night people you never saw during the day.

I gunned the Merc a little until I'd left that area behind. In front of me there were now fewer cars parked in the streets and I knew I was entering the more residential area. Here, the big, flashy Cadillacs and Pontiacs were either stashed away in lock-up garages or parked on wide driveways behind locked gates. The houses were all set back from the road, discreetly out of sight from other residents behind screens of trees.

I deliberately drove past the address I'd been given and parked on the opposite side of the road. Switching off the ignition, I got out and pulled up the collar of my overcoat. Lighting a cigarette, I drew on it while I gave the Galecci place the once-over.

There were a couple of big iron gates facing the street and a wide gravel drive leading up to the house. It had been built in the old Colonial style with white stone columns on either side of the front door. Lights still shone in several of the windows and there were four cars parked directly in front.

It looked about as impregnable as Fort Knox.

Tossing the cigarette butt into a puddle, I watched it wink out, then walked across. Just as I drew level with the gates, a couple of guys appeared out of nowhere and stood looking at me. The expressions on their faces said I'd better be there on business and not some nosy pedestrian.

The taller of the two said, 'You Johnny Merak?' His voice sounded like metal being sharpened on stone.

'That's right,' I replied, trying not to look as nervous as I felt.

'Mister Rizzio wants to see me. Said it was urgent and I was to come over right away.'

A pause and then the other guy pressed something at the side of the entrance and the gates slid aside. Once inside, the big guy frisked me like a professional and relieved me of the .38 nestling in my shoulder holster.

'Hey, is that necessary?' I asked. 'I feel naked without that.'

'You'll get it back when you leave,' he grated. 'Now follow me.'

There seemed no point in arguing any further. So long as I was on that side of those gates, I did as I was told if I valued my health.

What I couldn't figure out was why it had been Rizzio who'd made that phone call. Galecci had made it perfectly clear he wanted any information I got given to him personally.

The way I saw it, if it wasn't some other mob in the Organization that wanted Galecci dead, the most logical suspect had to be Rizzio. That was the way these people normally operated. After a while, men like him would get tired of playing second fiddle and want the top job for themselves and it was seldom they had the patience to wait until the boss died of natural causes.

Then there wasn't much time to consider such possibilities. We had reached the imposing front door. When it opened, I expected Rizzio to be there to welcome me but instead it was a flunkey, one of the house staff.

Without a word, he led me along a wide corridor. Here, the walls were lined with paintings, all of which appeared to be originals. Evidently Galecci was some kind of art collector and he certainly knew his stuff. None of this was trash. I figured there wasn't a single painting there which hadn't set him back less than a hundred grand.

The guy in the monkey suit showed me into a room at the far end of the corridor. There was a massive colonial desk in the middle of the room but there was nobody sitting behind it. I'd thought Rizzio would be there to give me the lowdown on why he wanted to see me in such a goddamned hurry. That, and the fact that apart from the manservant there didn't seem to be anyone else around, made me nervous.

Something was clearly going on here that I didn't understand and I certainly didn't like the feel of. I took the opportunity to examine the room.

If this was Galecci's office, like the pictures on the walls, it showed he had real taste. I had to give him that. Rich, thick carpet; hand-carved chairs, heavy plush drapes across the windows. He probably claimed it all back from tax as expenses for entertaining his rich business clients, I reckoned.

Just at that moment, the door at my back opened. I turned quickly. It was Rizzio and he didn't look too pleased.

'Merak,' he acknowledged with a slight inclination of his head. He made no attempt to shake hands or motion me to a chair.

'I gather you want to see me,' I said. 'You got something on your mind?'

He brushed a hand over his black, slicked-back hair. He seemed even more nervous than I was and that was a bad sign.

'I understand Mister Galecci hired you to do a job for him,' he said smoothly. 'Do

7

you mind telling me what it is?'

'I'd sure like to tell you,' I said. 'But client confidentiality, you know. All of that is between Mister Galecci and me.'

'No; it's between you and me now.' His voice seemed to snap little sparks. 'Things may have changed. At the moment, we're trying to find out if anything has happened to Mister Galecci. Now, I'm asking you again. What is it you've to do for him?'

I had the funny feeling in my bones that something really drastic had happened to my client and I wasn't sure just how much Rizzio was prepared to tell me. At the moment, he was calling the shots. There seemed nothing to do but go with the flow and hope to pick up some information on the way.

Shrugging, I said, 'Okay. He had this idea that somebody no longer wanted him in this world. He'd no idea who it was, which is why he hired me to poke around a little and see what I could come up with.'

'And have you come up with anything?'

'Not much so far. A man like him

makes a lot of enemies on the way to the top. It's a case of narrowing down any suspects. A process of elimination.'

He seemed to be turning that over in his mind, studying me closely to see if I might be holding anything back from him.

Then he shrugged and seemed to reach a decision. Jerking his head, he said, 'You'd better come with me.'

I followed him out of the room, wondering what was coming next. Through another large room and then he took me down a flight of stairs and here there were plenty of people milling around and a whole hive of activity. There was also a sharp smell in the air which I didn't recognize until I'd taken in everything that was going on.

Set in the far wall was a massive steel door, exactly the kind you'd find in a bank vault. A guy was crouched over an oxy-acetylene torch and was using it to burn through the six-inch thick steel around the lock. Several others were crowded round him,

'Just what the hell's going on?' I asked

Rizzio. I didn't really expect any answer but he gave one.

'That's Galecci's private vault. It's where he keeps most of his cash and also his collection of antique clocks,' he explained. 'That's another hobby of his like the paintings.'

From the way he said it, I gathered Rizzio didn't think much of either of these pastimes.

He went on, 'He goes in there every night at precisely eleven-fifteen and comes out again a couple of hours later. Everything precisely on the dot. But this time he hasn't.'

'You reckon he's still in there?'

'That's right.'

'How do you know he hasn't come out some time ago and locked the place up again?'

'Because there's no sign of him anywhere in the buildings. If he'd gone out, I'd have known about it.'

'So you figure something's happened to him. Doesn't anyone else have the combination?'

Rizzio stared at me as if I'd just uttered

something blasphemous. 'No one else has it. That's why we had to call in this guy to burn a way through.'

The guy with the torch suddenly snapped it off and stepped back. 'We're through, Mister Rizzio,' he said.

'Good. Everybody stay right where they are,' Rizzio ordered. He turned to a small, white-haired man. 'I want you to come in with me, doctor,' he said.

'And you as well, Merak.'

Grabbing the handle of the door, Rizzio pulled hard. Nothing happened for a few seconds, then the door swung open on well-oiled hinges. I followed him and the doctor inside, blinking in the harsh glare of the overhead strip lights.

The vault was bigger than I'd anticipated and the first thing I noticed were the clocks of all sizes and shapes ranged around the walls. There must have been hundreds of them.

The second thing was the table near the middle of the room with the solitary chair and its occupant. I knew right away it was Galecci and that he would no longer be needing my services. The handle of a knife protruded from between his shoulder blades and he was very dead.

I said nothing while the doctor examined him. But my mind was suddenly whirring inside my head like an overloaded engine. What I was seeing here didn't make any sense.

Rizzio moved towards the body and put one hand out towards the knife, then jerked his head around as I stopped him. 'Don't touch that. The police will want to dust it for fingerprints and you don't want yours all over it.'

There was a large metal box on the table directly in front of the body. Even from where I stood, I reckoned it contained a few hundred thousand dollars. Obviously whoever had killed him, robbery wasn't the motive.

But right at that moment, motive was the last thing on my mind. It was how the murder had been committed that I couldn't figure out.

Rizzio had been absolutely certain that Galecci came here alone around eleven-fifteen and left some two hours later, regular as clockwork. Even if someone had been waiting for him with a knife inside the vault, where was the killer now? Galecci would have locked the door immediately he was inside and I'd seen enough to know it would need the combination to open again from the inside.

There were certainly no places I could see where the killer might hide.

No windows through which he could have gone. The only exit was through that massive door and he certainly hadn't gone out that way.

Maybe it was a good thing that Galecci had been the one to hire me. I certainly didn't want to have to investigate this particular murder. It just didn't seem possible that anyone could have done it, inside a locked vault with only one way in and out, and only the dead man knowing the combination.

Rizzio waited impatiently until the doctor had finished his examination, then asked, 'Any idea when he died?'

'As near as I can put it, somewhere around midnight. Certainly not much later.'

'But how?' For once, Rizzio seemed at a loss for words.

'You tell me,' muttered the doctor. I had to hand it to the little guy, he didn't let Rizzio scare him. 'I'm just telling you the obvious. Someone stuck that knife in his back around midnight. Death was virtually instantaneous. Now the rest is up to the police. If they want me to make a statement, I will. But don't ask me how anybody got in and out of this place in order to kill him.'

Rizzio swung on me. 'You got any ideas, Merak?'

I shook my head. 'None, right now. But there are a couple of questions. Did anyone actually see him go into the vault last night? And has it remained closed all night?'

Rizzio signaled to one of the guys standing in the vault doorway, beckoning him in. Tersely, he asked him the same questions. The man nodded each time.

'Keller stays on guard outside the vault all the time the boss is in there. Nobody has gone in or come out since Galecci went in alone some seven hours ago.'

I could see that Rizzio was just as puzzled as I was. Unless you believed in the invisible man who could walk through six-inch thick steel walls, Galecci should have been as alive as we were!

I made a move towards the door. 'It looks as though Galecci won't be needing me any more,' I said. 'And unless you want to hire me to — '

He cut me off quickly. 'There won't be any further need for your services, Merak,' he said tonelessly. 'This is obviously a matter for the police now. And if any more has to be done in the light of their findings, I can take care of that myself.' Almost as an afterthought, he added, 'You know your way out.'

I shrugged. If that was the way he wanted it, it was fine by me. Frankly, I had the feeling that a certain Lieutenant Charles Donovan wouldn't be too pleased with this case either.

I pushed my way through the guys blocking the vault entrance and made my way back to the front door. All in all, it seemed I had just wasted my time coming here. The only reason that stood out in my mind at that moment, was that Rizzio had wanted me there as an independent witness once they discovered Galecci's body. It seemed odd he hadn't asked me in detail about anything I'd uncovered over the past three days. Maybe, now that Carlos Galecci was dead, that didn't matter any more.

I'd almost reached the front door when someone called my name. My hand went automatically for the .38 and then stopped as I remembered it was no longer there. Besides, I suddenly realized it was a woman's voice and when she stepped out of the shadows of the side corridor, I knew I wouldn't be needing my gun.

I recognized her right away. I'd seen pictures of her in the glossy magazines around the time she'd married Galecci. She'd been Gloria Benton then, I recalled. Some kind of model, small-time, posing for the usual run of photographers and trying to get into the movies. A statuesque blonde with vivid blue eyes, standing over six feet in her nylons, with a body to match.

Now she was dressed in a white sweater

and shorts and certainly not looking like the grieving widow to me.

'I have to talk with you, Mister Merak,' she said in a low, husky voice. 'It's important.'

After what I'd seen in that vault, I figured this might provide a pleasant diversion and followed her along the short corridor into the room near the end.

The place was fitted out as a gymnasium with all of the usual gimmicks; exercise machines, weights, climbing bars. I guessed it had been done for her benefit. Galecci hadn't looked the kind of guy who took much trouble over his physical shape. She closed the door behind us.

'Okay,' I said. 'What is it you want to see me about?'

Without answering, she walked towards the middle of the gym. There was a barbell on the floor and she came to a halt a little way from it, her back to it. Smiling a little, she performed a graceful back bend, hooking her hands under the bar. She held the pose for several seconds as I stood there, wondering what was coming next. Then she drew in a deep breath that did wonders for the sweater and straightened up, seemingly effortlessly, until she was standing, holding the weight over her head.

Somehow, I managed to pop my eyes back into their sockets.

She stood there for a full minute, the faintly supercilious smile on her full lips, before lowering the barbell slowly to the floor.

Standing back, she motioned towards it. I got my hands around it and tugged hard. I only managed to get it to my knees. It was the real McCoy all right and I guessed it weighed close on a hundred and fifty pounds.

Straightening up, I said harshly, 'Okay, Mrs Galecci. But you didn't ask me to come here just to show me how strong you are.'

She sobered instantly. 'No, you're right. I know my husband's been murdered. One of Rizzio's men told me just before I met you. Has Rizzio hired you to find his killer?'

'No,' I shook my head. 'He's leaving it in the hands of the police.'

'Good. Then you're hired.'

'Hey, hold on a minute,' I said. 'I've seen what's in that vault. This isn't the kind of case I'm interested in. Finding errant husbands is one thing, but a murder that's impossible is another. Rizzio made it clear he only wants the police in on this. He's already been in touch with Lieutenant Donovan of Homicide, I gather.'

'I'm not interested in Donovan, or the police. Most of them are fools and the others will do exactly as Rizzio tells them. Whatever Carlos offered you, I'll double it.'

'You want me to find out who killed your husband? Is that it?'

'That — and something more. I have good reason to believe that whoever did it, wants me dead too.'

'Now why should you think that?'

'Because Carlos left a will before he died. He left everything to me. Everything. I own all of this as of now, the whole operation. I'm asking you to help me because I need someone I can trust implicitly.'

I could see Rizzio wasn't going to be too pleased when he heard this. I wondered if he'd known about the existence of this will beforehand. If so, it put him a little lower on my list of suspects. It also put Gloria Galecci right at the top.

Even though she'd only just been told of her husband's departure from this world, her obvious lack of grief certainly didn't seem like the result of shock. And somehow I doubted if she had the ability and know-how to run an organization like this. Galecci had had his finger in every racket in LA.

'There's one thing worrying me,' I said. 'Why me? I'm just a one-man team, apart from Dawn Grahame, my secretary. You could surely afford one of the biggest agencies in town. They could put several men on the case, get results a lot quicker.'

She shook her head vehemently, the long blonde hair dancing across her bare shoulders. 'That's not what I want. All of that means organization, someone doing this and someone else doing that. I want a one-man team, someone personal I can contact at any time of the day or night.'

There was a double meaning to her last words and I saw something in her eyes that told me it was deliberate.

'So you're offering a two thousand dollar retainer plus expenses,' I said. 'And Gloria Galecci thrown in for good measure.'

The faint smile came back onto her lips as she said. 'That too, if you want it.'

'I may take you up on that sometime,' I replied. 'But right now, I'd like to ask you one question. It's personal. Where will Rizzio fit in now that Carlos has gone and you intend to take over?'

'If you're asking me whether there's ever been anything between Sam and me, the answer's — no.'

She sounded neither indignant nor mad at the question so I figured she might just be telling the truth.

'Okay, I'll take the job,' I told her. I knew it was a stupid thing to do and I'd probably regret it later.

'Somehow, I thought you would. I

know your office number. I'll ring you sometime every other day to see if you've found out anything.'

'And if I should ever need to get in touch with you?'

'I'd rather you didn't — not for a couple of weeks until I've got everything sorted out. You know how these lawyers are.'

I could guess. Rizzio wasn't going to take this lying down. He'd doubtless get some slick city lawyer to try to break the will. Things could turn really nasty.

From her tone, I guessed this meeting was at an end. She accompanied me to the front door. Rizzio was already there with a couple of his henchmen. He gave me a funny look but said nothing although I could almost hear his thoughts whirring away inside his head.

The rain had stopped and it was just getting light when I left. Just as I started along the drive, the gates opened and a police car drove in. It stopped in front of the house a couple of yards away and Lieutenant Charles Donovan got out. His official title was Lieutenant of the

Homicide Division, a big-sounding name and one he tried to live up to.

He saw me right away and the permanent scowl on his face deepened still further. 'Just what the hell are you doing here, Merak?' he demanded.

'You'd better ask Sam Rizzio that,' I replied calmly.

'He phoned me a couple of hours ago and asked me to get out here right away. Guess he knew that something had happened to his boss.'

Donovan snorted. 'Rizzio ain't your usual kind of client. You're getting a little outa your league, ain't you?'

I ignored the sarcasm. 'Matter of fact, it was Carlos Galecci who hired me in the first place three days ago. Reckoned then that someone was out to get him.'

His lips curled back in what was meant to be a humorous smile, showing his teeth. 'Seems you weren't all that good at your job then, from what I've just been informed. If Galecci is dead, I reckon your part in this case is finished.'

'Now that would've made your day, Lieutenant,' I said. 'But I've just been rehired.'

'Oh.' Donovan looked hard and inquiringly at Rizzio who shook his head.

'So who's hired you?'

'It's no secret, I guess. Mrs Galecci.'

That shook him a little but he swiftly regained his composure. 'Well just keep out of my hair, that's all. And you uncover any real evidence, you pass it on to me right away. Got that?'

He brushed past me, said something in a low voice to Rizzio, then went into the house with Sergeant Kowolinsky trailing after him.

I picked up my gun from the guy at the gate, checked it was still loaded, and slipped it into its holster before walking back to my car.

Getting in, I settled behind the wheel for a while, turning things over in my mind. I still wasn't sure I'd done the right thing, agreeing to work for Gloria Galecci. From what I'd seen, there was no possible way anyone could have killed Galecci. Unless he'd somehow managed to stick that knife in the middle of his back himself, the whole thing looked impossible.

What Donovan would make of it, I didn't know. He wasn't the most imaginative of men when it came to solving murders like this.

Give him some body stretched out in an alley with plenty of prints and clues lying around and he was in his element. But with an impossible murder like this seemed to be and with Rizzio breathing down the back of his neck, I couldn't see him making much of it.

I drove back to my office slowly, hitting the early morning traffic for most of the way. Dawn Grahame was just opening up when I got there. She eyed me curiously. Normally I arrived no earlier than nine and it must have been obvious to her that I'd been up for some time.

'Don't tell me you've been out all night on a case, Johnny,' she said as I slumped down in my chair behind the desk.

I nodded. 'Get me some coffee, Dawn. Black and as strong as you can make it.'

She came back with it five minutes later. After seating herself on the edge of the desk, she asked, 'This got something to do with Carlos Galecci?'

'Carlos is dead,' I told her, sipping the coffee. It burned my tongue and the back of my throat but it brought some of the warmth and feeling back into my chilled body. 'They found him this morning. The doc reckons he died some time around midnight.'

'But not of natural causes?'

'Not exactly. We found him inside a locked vault with a knife in his back. They had to burn through the lock to get inside.'

Dawn whistled faintly through her teeth. She brought out a small file and began working on her nails. After a moment's reflection, she said. 'And you're absolutely sure he died inside that vault?'

I could see what she was getting at, the same possibility had occurred to me when I first saw the body. Had someone knifed Galecci just as he'd opened the vault, carried him inside and set him up in that chair, before letting themselves out, closing the door behind them?

'I see what you mean, Dawn. The same idea had occurred to me. But he was seen going inside at his usual time and there

26

was nothing out of the ordinary then.'

She thought that over for a moment before pronouncing her considered verdict. 'Then I guess you're faced with something that couldn't possibly have happened.'

'Just what I told Sam Rizzio.'

'All right. So where do you fit in now that Galecci's dead? Has Rizzio hired you to find the killer?'

'Not Rizzio. Mrs Galecci.'

Dawn gave me an enigmatic look. 'You're working for her?'

'That's about it.' I finished the coffee. 'The trouble is, I don't even know where to start. I'd like to get a good look around that vault but I reckon that's out of the question. And I'm damned sure Donovan won't talk to me. The guy hates my guts.'

'Is there no one else on the case who'll talk to you?' Dawn got up and walked across to the window.

I mulled that over. I knew a few of the officers in the Homicide Squad. A few of them were decent guys. But they all took their orders from Donovan and whether any would give me any information was problematical. Still, it was worth a try.

'There's Jack Kolowinski,' I said. 'He was with Donovan this morning. Once he's off duty, I guess I know where to find him.'

Kowolinski was unmarried, and he'd helped me on a couple of cases before. A decent cop but a little too addicted to the hard stuff. He'd been in the force almost twenty-five years and would certainly have made promotion a long time ago had it not been for his drinking.

'Anything you'd like me to do?' Dawn asked.

'Find out anything you can on Galecci. Somebody wanted him dead and whoever it was, they certainly picked a unique way of doing it. They must have known his routine and somehow they had access to that vault.'

'I'll get on to it right away.'

'And run a check on Sam Rizzio, though I doubt if you'll find much.'

2

Seven o' clock that evening and I was standing outside Mancini's Bar. It was one of those places midway between Skid Row and the upper class joints near the middle of town. Folk went there for a quiet drink, to forget their troubles, or to pour them out to anyone stupid enough to listen.

It was also the place that Jack Kolowinsky frequented most. At weekends, when he was off duty, he'd sometimes drive out into the country but during the week he would be here, sitting at the end of the bar furthest from the door, his backside on a stool and his hand clamped around a glass.

He was there, just as I'd figured, when I pushed my way through the doors. Five foot ten, starting to gray at the temples. He'd seen more than his share of violence, bodies lying in alleys or pulled out of the river with concrete shoes, to last a lifetime. Someday, if he kept his nose clean, he'd spend a couple of years sitting behind a desk, pushing papers, filing reports. Then he'd retire to a nice little place in the suburbs. If the booze didn't get him first.

The place was smoky. On a clear day you could sometimes make out the far wall as you stepped inside. The lighting wasn't too brilliant either. But that was how the clientele liked it and Mancini saw no reason to put good money into fancy lighting when most of his customers preferred the anonymity of shadows.

I strolled over and seated myself on the stool next to his. He knew I was there but he didn't turn his head.

'Hello, Jack,' I said.

He finished whatever was in his glass and set it down on the counter in front of him. 'What do you want, Johnny?'

'Now why should I want anything, Jack? Can't a guy come in for a quiet drink with an old friend?'

He sighed. His gaze remained fixed on the empty glass.

I nodded to the barkeep. 'Same again

for him,' I said. 'Whiskey on the rocks for me.'

When the drinks came, I waited until he'd taken a couple of slugs from his before saying, 'There is something you could do for me, Jack.'

'I knew it. Don't you guys ever do any leg works for yourselves?'

I ignored that. 'You're working with Donovan on the Galecci case. I saw you with him this morning.'

'So?' There was no expression on his sad face. He was still staring at the glass in his hand as if hoping there might be another miracle like that at Caana.

'Mrs. Galecci has hired me to find out who killed her husband. There are some things I've got to know and I'm damned sure your boss won't tell me a thing. The same goes for Sam Rizzio.'

He pushed himself a little way from the bar and rubbed his back. 'If you're asking me to get you access to the murder scene, forget it. There's no way I can do that.'

'That's not what I'm asking, Jack. I managed to get a good look around while I was there with Rizzio. But you saw the set-up. While Galecci had locked himself inside that vault, nobody could get to him and knife him.'

He nodded ponderously. 'Damnedest thing I ever saw in all my years with Homicide. Donovan's stumped, I can tell you that.'

'What about Rizzio? You got any files on him?'

He swung round a little on his stool to face me for the first time. 'You want me to lose my job? I can't give out any information like that without Donovan's say-so.'

'Which you're not likely to get.' I said pointedly. 'Donovan hates me like poison. I give you my word, anything you say goes no further than this bar.'

He sat silent for a little while, then tossed down the rest of the liquor without flinching and pushed the empty glass in my direction. I lifted a finger to the barkeep who filled up the glass once more.

'Okay, Johnny,' he muttered finally. His words were now becoming a trifle slurred. I wanted him to have just enough liquor to loosen his tongue, but not enough for him to start talking to me from the floor.

'We got a file as big as your fist on Rizzio. Came over from Sicily some fifteen years ago. Nothing big at first. A couple of robberies, a few stolen cars. Then he started in on the drugs racket. That's when he came to the notice of Carlos Galecci. There's been plenty since then including at least three murders, but none of them stuck. Some smart lawyer, hired by Galecci no doubt, got him off every time. Now that he's top man, it'll be even harder to pin anything on him.'

I nodded. Evidently he didn't know anything about what Gloria had told me that morning, that Rizzio might no longer be top dog.

I switched the topic of conversation. 'What's your opinion of Mrs. Galecci?'

This time, his deadpan expression did change, to one of surprise. I could see he was wondering why I'd asked that question.

'I thought she's the one who hired you this morning?'

'She is. But I also like to know

something about those who employ me, just for my own protection, you know. These days you can't be too careful. And I prefer to know things from an independent source.'

'Not much I can tell you there apart from what's common knowledge. She's clean as far as we are concerned. We've got nothing on her at all, not even a parking ticket. Small-time model who never made it into Hollywood. Guess she landed on her feet when she married Galecci.'

'You reckon she's smart enough to commit murder?'

'Maybe. She didn't get to being where she is now by being dumb.'

'You figure she's smart enough to run that entire organization?'

'Hell — no! What gave you that fool idea?'

'Something she told me this morning. Seems Galecci left everything to her in his will. And she's determined to be the boss.'

Jack's face changed abruptly at that. It was almost as if some other guy was sitting on the stool next to me.

'If she tried a stunt like that, there's going to be hell to pay,' he said finally. 'I know Rizzio. He won't stand for any dame taking over and giving him orders.'

'That's the way I figured it.' I nodded to the barkeep who placed another glass on the bar and poured more liquor into it without spilling a drop. 'I guess Donovan questioned Rizzio and Gloria this morning. You reckon he knows anything about this?'

'If he does, he said nothing to me.'

I got down from my stool. 'Just one other thing, Jack. Have you managed to find out how many people have had access to that vault apart from Galecci?'

'Quite a few unfortunately, but never alone. Galecci was always with them.'

'Give me a few names.'

'Mrs Galecci, of course. Sam Rizzio and a guy named Foran. He's some kind of accountant, checks the books every now and again.'

'Thanks,' I said. 'You've been a great help. I owe you one.'

'Yeah.' He picked up the glass that had

just been filled. 'I'll remember that when the time comes.'

Leaving him slumped over the bar, I made for the door, wondering how he ever made it to work in the mornings.

Outside, the fresh air hit me like a fist after the atmosphere inside the bar.

Unlike the previous night, the sky was clear and there was a yellow slice of moon, like a piece of melon, hanging low towards the west. I walked slowly towards the spot where I'd parked the Merc a couple of blocks away.

There weren't too many folk around on the sidewalks. Those who worked during the day in the city were gone and the night people hadn't come out yet.

I turned the corner of the second block. My car was parked at the kerb just where I'd left it. There was another immediately behind it, a black limousine with a guy seated behind the wheel. The engine was running and I guess that should have started the alarm bells ringing in my mind.

I reached for the .38 but I was too slow. I'd expected a couple of hoods to come bursting out of the back of the limousine. Instead, there was a sudden quiet sound at my back and then the cold muzzle of a gun was pushed hard against the back of my neck. A hand slid across my shoulder and removed my gun and a voice said, 'Don't try any heroics Merak, and you may not get hurt. Now move!'

I moved and the muzzle of the gun kept pace with me as I walked towards the black limousine.

The rear door popped open without anybody touching it.

'Inside,' said the voice.

I got into the back, sliding across to the middle of the plush seat as the guy with the gun climbed in beside me. A second man got in the other door, crushing in on my other side.

'You mean to tell me where we're going?' I asked.

'You'll find that out soon enough,' said the guy on my right. The way he said it told me I'd get no answers to any further questions and if I knew what was good for me, I'd keep quiet.

There was no sound from the engine as

we pulled away from the kerb into the main stream of early-night traffic. I watched the dim shape of the Merc slide smoothly past and wondered when I'd see it again. Whoever these guys were, they weren't playing games.

We curved through the streets towards the outskirts of town, driving north. The driver sat easy behind the wheel. He could have been asleep for all I knew but he passed all of the other drivers as if they'd been standing still.

Once we slid past a police patrol car, traveling at well over seventy, but there was no siren or flashing lights on our tail. Whoever owned this particular car was well known to the cops and, for some reason, they turned a blind eye to it.

We hit the outskirts less than ten minutes later, leaving all of the colored lights of LA behind us. In front of us was only darkness, the gray ribbon of the road, and the moon just touching the tops of the foothills.

Then the road dipped, twisted like a rattler's back, before straightening out again. The car slowed slightly and then swung left onto a much narrower road with the tires making a little more noise now on loose stones. Obviously, wherever I was being taken, there would be few spectators around to hear any screams. Not a light showed anywhere. It was as dark as the inside of a grave and about as funny.

A nasty thought occurred to me, sitting there like the ham in a sandwich.

Either I was being taken for a ride to someplace where nobody would ever find me, or I was to meet with someone — and whoever it was, they certainly didn't like company or nosy neighbors. Either way, it churned my stomach into knots. Since going straight, I'd had little contact with the various mobs who made up the Organization. Now, after being hired first by Galecci and then by his widow, I could be in deep trouble up to my neck.

We were still doing well over seventy, driving to the end of the world in almost total darkness with only the twin headlights picking out the bumps and twists in the road. Whoever the driver was, he'd have made it big-time on any racing circuit in the world.

Then, suddenly, there were lights in front of us. We'd topped the brow of a high hill and the tiny cluster of lights appeared down below us. An acutely-angled bend showed briefly at the bottom of the hill and somehow we got round it without skidding off the road. There were a couple of gates fifty yards in front and fortunately they were open and we glided through them, coasting along a wide drive before coming to a smooth halt at the side of a massive building, all red brick and glass.

The guy on my left got out and motioned me to do likewise. He went around to the rear of the mansion. Clearly, private eyes and the like were supposed to use the tradesmen's entrance. The front door was reserved for the elite of LA.

The door opened just as we reached it and I could imagine a red neon sign over it saying: 'Abandon all hope all ye who enter here'.

Inside, the big guy walked ahead of me

to an elevator at the end and pushed a button on the wall. I guess he figured I wasn't dumb enough to try anything because he never even looked at me as I followed him into the square opening. The door closed and we were rising smoothly into the upper levels of the place.

When it stopped, we were inside a large room, tastefully furnished in the Oriental style; thick Persian rugs on the floor and the biggest desk I had ever seen with a couple of shaded lamps standing like sentinels at either end. There was no one in the room but the silence held a hint that somebody had either been there only a little while before, or would soon come in. While the bruiser stood silently beside me, I scanned the corners of the walls for any cameras that might be focused on me, studying my reactions for the benefit of someone in another room.

I couldn't see any, but that went for nothing. Whoever owned this place had more than enough dough to have these very cleverly concealed. I stopped trying and turned to my friendly companion.

'Do you mind telling me why I've been brought here?'

'You'll find that out soon enough,' he muttered. He deliberately kept his voice low as if scared of being overheard talking to me.

I stood there for almost five minutes with the feeling that this waiting was deliberate, that someone out of sight was sizing me up. Then a door at the side of the room slid noiselessly open and a man stepped into the room. Maybe 'stepped' is the wrong word. Rather he waddled in; a huge guy not more than five-five in height but almost the same around. I knew who he was even before he went to the desk and somehow eased his considerable bulk into the large, high-backed chair behind it.

Enrico 'The Boss' Manzelli, head of the entire LA Organization. Here was the real power behind the mobs.

The lamps on the desk had been so arranged that his face remained in shadow but I knew he was watching me closely from beneath the heavy lids. The FBI had tried to get him once on some charge or other and that was the only time he'd ever appeared on the front pages. He was a man who basked in the shadows, scarcely ever leaving this huge mansion miles from anywhere. But it was from here that the orders went out; orders that were always obeyed without question.

He waved a thick-fingered hand in my direction. 'Please sit down, Mister Merak.' His voice had that Sydney Greenstreet chuckle with the distinct undertone of menace. 'I apologize for bringing you here like this, but we have to talk.'

I sat down nervously on the edge of the chair, facing him across the desk. I had the feeling that my situation was, at best, extremely precarious.

It wasn't like Manzelli to take an interest in small-time guys like me unless it was something pretty important. I guessed I hadn't inadvertently done something he didn't like, otherwise I'd have been at the bottom of the sea by now, staring at the fishes.

'Go ahead,' I said, trying to speak as

evenly as possible. 'What is it you want to talk about?'

'Gloria Galecci,' he said softly. 'You may say that she's posed a problem for me. I am in a very sensitive position although I don't expect you to know anything about that. I have to maintain some kind of order among many businesses in this town, otherwise there would be anarchy, a return to the bad old days of the twenties. As you may imagine, it isn't easy with so many different people competing for different things.'

'I can imagine,' I said. 'But I don't see where Mrs Galecci comes into this. Her husband's just been murdered and — '

'My dear Mister Merak,' he interrupted without any inflexion in his voice. 'I am not a fool. Everything that goes on in this town, I know about almost before it happens. Carlos Galecci was a good man, but he was stupid to have made that will. Had I known about that, it would never have happened.'

He sighed dramatically and leaned forward over the desk as far as his stomach would allow.

'So where do I come in?' I asked. 'After all, the only contact I've ever had with Galecci, or his wife, was when he hired me because he was so sure that he was on somebody's hit list.'

Manzelli made an impatient gesture with his left hand. Then he placed both hands together and stared at me over the fleshy pyramid.

'The very fact that you did come into contact with them means I have to take an interest in you. Gloria Galecci has hired you to find whoever killed her husband. What she really wants from you is to kill Sam Rizzio. So long as he's alive, she has no chance of taking over that group.'

'I'm no hitman,' I said. 'I don't set out to kill men in cold blood, not even men like Rizzio.'

Nothing much changed in Manzelli's expression. His well-manicured nails made a little tattoo on the desk. A faint smile twitched across the thick lips and his double chins moved slightly above the tight collar of his starch-white shirt.

'Sometimes, women can get men to do

things they'd rather not,' he said mean-ingfully. 'Particularly women like Gloria Galecci. She didn't get to be where she is now by just using her brains.'

'No — I guess not.' Right at that moment, I believed him. I began to revise my opinion of Gloria.

'However,' Manzelli's tone changed. It was now as hard as an iron bar. 'Think over what I've said about her. Now to get to the reason I invited you here at such short notice. I've no objection to you trying to find Galecci's killer. As far as that's concerned, you can go along with your investigations. My interest is in Rizzio. I have certain plans in mind for him and I won't allow anything to change them. Should anything unfortu-nate happen to him, I may have to take some action against those I feel may be responsible.'

There was no doubt in my mind what he meant, who he was referring to.

Gloria Galecci and myself. I figured he'd already made up his mind I was in cahoots with her to remove Rizzio from the equation.

'You get my meaning, Merak?' His gaze bored so deeply into me I could almost feel it scratching away at the back of my skull.

'Sure. I've got it perfectly,' I said.

'Good. One other thing. This may only be a hunch, but I have a gut-feeling in here,' he tapped the side of his head, 'that there's someone else involved in this murder. I don't think either Rizzio or Gloria did it. It isn't their style. But whoever killed Carlos in that locked vault is a highly dangerous man. That's why I want you to stay on the job. You've cracked some difficult cases in the past. I'm sure you can come up with the answer to this one.'

'If I should get any ideas, should I come to you with them?'

He shook his head ponderously. 'After tonight, you'll have no communication with me. Mario here will call on you now and again. You can give any information you have to him.'

'Fine,' I said. In the position I was in, there was nothing else to say.

One wrong word, one wrong gesture,

that Manzelli didn't like and I'd have no more chance of getting back to LA than running for President.

'Good.' He signaled to the big guy still standing like a statue somewhere in the background. 'Mario will see that you get back to where you left your car.'

I got up. The soulless eyes followed me. 'Goodnight, Mister Merak. I sincerely hope we never meet again.'

'I'll drink to that,' I said.

The shiny black limousine was where we'd left it, only this time it was facing in the other direction. The same mute driver sat impassively behind the wheel, staring straight ahead. As I climbed into the back, I wondered if he ate and slept in that position in the car.

The drive back was a replica of the outward journey in reverse. The car slid to a smooth halt just opposite mine. I got out and stood on the sidewalk

The big guy leaned out of the window and handed my gun back. From the weight of it, I knew it was still loaded. Once the twin tail lights had vanished into the night, I walked across to the

Merc and got in.

I felt like a stiff drink and Mancini's was just a stone's throw away, the neon light a siren call. But that would have numbed my mind and right now I needed to think, clearly and coherently.

Mentally turning down the offer of a drink, I drove back to my apartment where I called Dawn.

'Where on earth did you get to, Johnny?' Her voice sounded sharp with concern. 'I tried to get you at Mancini's but he said you'd been talking to Jack Kolowinsky and had then left.'

'I had an appointment I didn't know about,' I said.

There was a pause, then, 'Who was this appointment with — or would you rather I minded my own business?'

'Nothing like that, Dawn. Some hoods picked me up in the street just after I left Mancini's and drove me out to Enrico Manzelli's place in the country.'

'Manzelli!' I picked out her sharp intake of breath and could almost hear her thoughts chasing themselves like mice inside her head. 'But he's — '

'Mister Bigshot himself. I know.'

'But what did he want with you?' She sounded a little frightened now.

'Not exactly champagne and caviare,' I said. 'He's trying to find out if I'm in with Gloria Galecci to pick off Sam Rizzio and that's something he doesn't want to happen. But he's just as anxious to find out who killed Galecci as I am.'

She didn't ask any more questions. Not that there was much more I could have told her. Instead, she said, 'I'll see you in the morning, Johnny. I've got some information on Rizzio and Mrs. Galecci that might interest you.'

The phone went dead.

I sat down in the big chair in front of the electric fire, stretched out my legs, and tried to figure out where I'd got to on this case. I didn't doubt that Manzelli was telling the truth when he'd suggested that Gloria might be plotting Rizzio's demise.

Certainly, he would prove to be the biggest stumbling block to her plans of taking over the organization her husband had built up in that area of LA.

Equally, she could have had a hand in

Carlos' murder. She was an ambitious woman, cold and calculating, determined to get everything she wanted and not particular as to how she went about it.

I was on the point of going to bed when the phone rang.

It was Donovan. He sounded mad.

'Merak?'

'Yeah. What's on your mind? I was just going to sleep. I've had a busy day.'

'I'll say you have.'

I could imagine him sitting behind his desk, snarling into the phone.

He paused, more for dramatic effect than to get his breath back. 'You've been talking to one of my men.'

'Oh?'

'That's right. You were in Mancini's holding a conference with Jack Kolowinsky.'

'Does he say that?'

'No. But I've had a tail on you all day. I figured you might try to pull a stunt like this.'

'A guy has to get his information from somewhere,' I said politely. I thought of some witty remarks to say, but reckoned they wouldn't go down too well with him in his present mood.

'This is a police case, damnit! A homicide. I warned you this morning to stay out of my hair. If there's any information to be given out, I'll give it when I'm good and ready. I don't want anyone, you in particular, going behind my back. Have you got that?'

'Got it, Charles,' I said evenly. I knew that using his first name would stoke up his anger even further but right then, I didn't give a damn. There were much bigger guys than Donovan on my back.

'Another thing,' he went on when he'd got himself under control. 'Just where did you go once you left Mancini's? Don't waste my time telling me you went back to your apartment because your car was parked just around the corner for a couple of hours and you weren't in it.'

I thought fast. Obviously, whoever had been tailing me hadn't seen those guys take me for a ride. 'Nowhere in particular,' I told him. 'Is it against the law now to walk around town?'

'Don't play funny games with me,

Merak. It wouldn't take much for me to have your license revoked.'

I knew he was bluffing just to provoke me into saying something I didn't want to say. My license had been issued by the state and that didn't put it under his jurisdiction. Maybe he could get someone higher up to do it, but he'd need a better excuse than non-cooperation.

'Let's try this one then,' I said. 'I met up with a couple of guys just around the corner from Mancini's. One of them had a gun. They took me out into the country to meet Manzelli. Just for a cosy chat, you understand. Once that was over to our mutual satisfaction, they brought me back.'

'Go to hell, Merak. And watch yourself from now on.' He sneered the threat angrily and hung up.

I knew he hadn't believed a word I'd said, and that was the way I wanted it.

Somehow, though, Galecci's murder had opened a big can of worms and right now they were wriggling all over LA.

3

Galecci's funeral was, by any standards, a showpiece, even for LA. The hearse was only a little shorter than a football field, suitably adorned with wreaths and flowers from every mob in the Organization. A score or so identical black limousines followed it like baby ducklings trooping after their mother.

News of his death had been given out to the media and there was quite a turnout of the local population to watch it go by. Newsreel cameras were positioned at every intersection along the route. Perhaps there were a few genuine mourners among the crowd but I doubted it. If there were, they were in the minority. The rest were probably glad to see him go.

I'd parked the Merc just inside the cemetery gates not wanting to appear conspicuous among the gathering. I'd asked Dawn to come with me. Not that she had any liking for such occasions but because, at times, a woman's intuition can be extremely useful and it had proved invaluable in the past.

As befitted the dismal scene, it was raining. A steady downpour that showed no sign of letting up. I guess some might have said the heavens were weeping for Galecci's passing. Me, I figured it was just God's way of saying we were all fools for coming.

Dawn and I found ourselves a suitable vantage point in the dubious shelter of a large elm tree as the cortege arrived, the cars lining themselves up with military precision. We weren't there to pay our respects to the dear departed. My reason for braving the inclement weather was far different.

There's an old saying that the murderer is always present at the victim's funeral and I wanted to get a good look at the faces of everyone present. I'd no idea who I was looking for. It was nothing more than a hunch that might just pay off.

Once they were all assembled at the graveside, I gave the entire gathering the once-over. The majority were people I'd have expected to be present. In the forefront, trying their best to look suitably somber for the occasion, were Sam Rizzio and Gloria Galecci. I could just make out Gloria's face behind the black veil but it was impossible to tell whether she was crying, or secretly smiling.

There was one guy, however, I didn't recognize. He was standing a little way back from the others as if he was a professional mourner and had just walked in from the street. He was dressed in a black, threadbare suit, his head bowed. He looked as much out-of-place as I felt.

He had a halo of pure white hair and a small, wrinkled face that was ageless. He could have been anywhere between fifty and ninety. He didn't have the look of the Organization about him and it was this that attracted my attention to him right away. Also, he was standing alone as if he hadn't a friend in the world.

Further back, standing among the trees, were two others keeping a watchful eye on the proceedings. Lieutenant Donovan and Sergeant Kolowinsky.

Both were doing their utmost to blend in with the background. I knew Donovan had spotted me and his mind was doubtless working overtime trying to figure out why the hell I was there.

'You think whoever killed Galecci is likely to be here?' Dawn asked in a low, guarded whisper.

'Anything's possible,' I said. 'It looks to me as though Donovan is thinking the same thing.'

'But even if the killer is here, among all these people, it could be anyone.'

'Sure. Even that little guy in the black suit yonder.' I inclined my head in his direction. 'I don't suppose you have any idea who he is?'

Dawn shook her head and brushed a strand of wet hair out of her eyes.

'I've never seen him before. But he doesn't look as though he could harm a fly.'

'Sometimes, that type make the best killers. Nobody suspects them. But whether he could or not, I'd sure like to know who he is and what he's doing here.'

At the graveside, the preacher's voice droned on and on, mouthing the usual eulogies, asking God to forgive Galecci's sins in this world and welcome his immortal soul into heaven. In his heart of hearts, he must have known that hell would surely claim it first.

I could feel the raindrops dripping in a veritable deluge down the back of my neck from the overhanging branches and told myself I'd probably be drier simply standing out in the rain.

The ceremony lasted no longer than twenty minutes. I reckon the preacher deliberately cut it short because he was getting wet like the rest of us.

After shaking hands with the assembly and offering his condolences to the widow, he left and the others began making their way towards the waiting cars.

Out of the corner of my eye, I noticed Donovan hurrying in Rizzio's direction with Kolowinsky trailing at his heels like a lost puppy. I didn't want either of them asking me any awkward questions right then. I had a lot of other things on my mind. But my sigh of relief never came because at that moment, Gloria let go of Rizzio's supporting arm and came towards me. There was a grim, hard expression on her face.

Donovan stopped abruptly a couple of feet away.

'Mister Merak,' she said. 'I was hoping to meet you.'

'Something bothering you?' I tried to analyze the look on her face.

'I've been thinking things over since we last met and I've come to the conclusion that it would be better if the investigation into my husband's death was left solely in the hands of the police. Naturally, I'll arrange for a suitable payment to be made to you for anything you've done so far.'

I knew right then there was something more to her statement than just wanting me off the case. Maybe it had something to do with the talk I'd had with Manzelli, maybe not.

'I guess you must have your reasons for this.' I gave what I hoped was a warm, friendly smile. 'But there's something niggling away at the back of my mind. Guess you'd say I'm a little too cynical for my own good. Okay, you no longer want to hire me.'

'That's right.'

I shrugged slightly. 'The trouble is, I still figure I owe something to your late husband. I wasn't able to stop him getting killed and he never got around to taking me off the case. So I sure as hell mean to find out who killed him — and how. That way, I'll earn that thousand dollars he gave me as a retainer.'

'You're being very foolish, Merak.' Donovan stepped forward and he gave me a look that should have killed me on the spot. 'You heard what Mrs. Galecci just said. She doesn't want you poking your nose in any longer. And that goes for me too.'

'Somehow, I thought it would.' I returned his stare with interest. 'You know, I'm wondering just why it is I'm suddenly a threat to everybody. Seems to me there are a lot of people who have a lot to hide.'

'You're not a threat,' Donovan said, his

voice as polite as that of a bouncer in one of the downtown nightclubs. 'Merely a nuisance. You're deliberately getting in the way of a murder investigation.'

'Not in the least,' I replied smoothly. 'I'm merely carrying out my original client's last wishes. You wouldn't deny a dead man that right, would you Lieutenant?'

'Go to hell, Merak,' he snarled viciously. 'Just step out of line once and I'll have you back in jail so fast you won't know what hit you.'

'I'll bear that in mind.'

I watched him strut after Rizzio and Gloria.

'That wasn't wise, Johnny.' Dawn looked concerned. 'You've made a real enemy of him now, not to mention Mrs. Galecci. They can do you a whole lot of harm if they try.'

She paused to see if I was going to say anything, then shook her head despairingly. 'Okay, where to now? Back to the office?'

'No.' I'd already ascertained that the little guy was still walking slowly across the grass, his head down against the wind and driving rain. 'I want to keep an eye on him, see where he goes.' I gave a brief nod in the man's direction. 'I've got to know who he is and what his connection was with Galecci. There's something about him that worries me and I've got an aversion to leaving loose ends hanging around. They have a way of getting all tangled up until they make a noose.'

By the time we reached the Merc, the old guy was climbing into a battered old Ford some fifty yards from us. I let Dawn drive. Right then, I had some serious thinking to do.

She switched on the ignition and waited until the Ford drove slowly past.

Expertly, she swung the Merc around in a tight turn and tailed him. The rest of the mourners had already departed. No doubt heading for the Galecci place where the usual banquet would be laid on for them and everybody would be saying what a great guy Carlos had been.

I hoped our quarry wasn't heading in the same direction but he swung left at the cemetery gates, keeping a steady pace.

It was impossible to lose him in the traffic as he led us through the middle of town and then out west.

Soon we were driving through the more squalid quarter of LA. Rows of small shops, some boarded up, delicatessens and derelict buildings lined each side of the mean streets.

It was quiet now with hardly any traffic. There was loneliness, despair and years of poverty written all over these streets and buildings. It was stamped indelibly on the faces of the few pedestrians on the sidewalks.

Dawn leaned forward a little over the wheel, easing her foot off the accelerator as the Ford slowed even further. 'You don't think he knows we're tailing him, do you? He seems to be driving nowhere.'

'If he is, then he's definitely connected to this case somewhere along the line,' I said. 'But right now I've no idea where he fits in.'

We followed the Ford along a narrow street that was little more than an alley and then came out onto a main thoroughfare. Ahead of us, the Ford suddenly slid to a halt in front of a dingy shop. Our man got out, unlocked the shop door, and went inside.

'Wait here,' I said.

I got out and walked towards the Ford, then glanced up at the name above the shop front. It read, in faded gilt letters: Anton Tefler. Clockmaker and Jeweler.

So that was where the little guy fitted in. He must have been a regular visitor to the Galecci place for a number of years, getting clocks from all over the world for Carlos' collection. Almost certainly Galecci had been one of his best customers and he, of all people, would have been sorry to see him go. That, at least, explained why he had attended the funeral.

Little mice started scampering around inside my head. It seemed unlikely, but was it possible this guy had anything to do with Galecci's murder? I couldn't see how or why but once the idea got into my mind, it stayed there.

The shop window was dust-smeared and rain-spattered. I couldn't make out much but the interior seemed to be filled with watches and clocks of every shape and size. It was just like the interior of Galecci's vault only on a much smaller scale.

I walked back to Dawn. 'He's a clockmaker,' I told her. 'And it figures he's the guy who got all of those that Galecci collected. Maybe if we turned a little heat on him, he might tell us something.'

Dawn got out and we went together to the door. A bell chimed somewhere as I pushed it open and went inside.

There was a constant din in the place. It hit me the moment I got through the door. Every single one of those clocks was going, ticking away the minutes and the seconds, each with its own particular sound. I checked my watch and saw that it was a little after eleven-fifteen. If they all chimed on the hour, the racket must have been deafening.

A low wooden counter stretched halfway along the room near one wall.

There was nobody behind it but a moment later a door at the back opened and the guy we had been following came through. There was no sign of recognition on his face but that counted for nothing.

Part of the counter had a dusty glass front that was meant to display trays of rings and bracelets. But not only was the glass dirty, as if it hadn't been cleaned for years, the lighting inside the shop was so bad it was virtually impossible to see them. Those I could make out, however, looked like the real thing. Diamonds, sapphires and rubies all set in gold. Where he got his customers for such expensive stuff was beyond me. Certainly not from anyone living in the neighborhood we'd just driven through.

Dawn bent and busied herself examining them.

'Are you looking for anything in particular?' Tefler asked. His voice was dry and soft, like leaves rustling in the wind. There was just the trace of an accent.

I took out my card and pushed it across the counter. He picked it up and squinted owlishly at it.

'John Merak.' He mouthed the words, then gave the card back. 'I don't understand. What has a private detective to do with me?'

'Maybe if I were to mention the name Carlos Galecci, it would help,' I said, watching his face closely for any reaction.

Something flickered briefly in his deep-set eyes.

When he said nothing, I went on, 'I reckon you must have known him pretty well before his unexpected demise. I noticed you at the funeral. My guess is that you helped with his collection, maybe purchased clocks from all over the world and then sold them on to him. At a good profit to yourself, of course.'

He didn't attempt to deny it. 'That is so. But there is no law against that. Unless you're suggesting any of them were stolen or obtained by other illegal methods. I can assure you that neither is true.'

'Oh, I believe you,' I said softly. 'I'm not investigating any thefts or illegal imports of antiques.' I leaned forward over the counter so that my face was only a couple of inches from his. 'I was hired by Carlos Galecci a few days ago. He figured somebody was out to kill him and wanted me to find out who it was.'

Tefler pulled his head away so fast he almost overbalanced. I knew I'd hit a nerve somewhere. All I had to do now was find it.

'Carlos is dead.' I could scarcely make out his words for the infernal ticking of the clocks. 'You know that. I know that. It means you no longer work for him and I don't think I should answer any more of your questions.'

'No?'

He still had that scared look about him but he was trying hard not to show it.

'No,' he echoed. 'And I should tell you I have good friends in the police department. Important friends. I don't have to answer any more of your questions.'

'No, you don't,' I agreed. 'And I suppose Lieutenant Donovan of Homicide is one of your good friends.'

He pressed his lips so tightly together they almost disappeared. I figured I wouldn't get much more out of him. I had just one more question for him, however.

'That clock collection Galecci had stashed away in that vault. Do you have any idea what's going to happen to it now? I don't suppose Mrs. Galecci will want to keep them.'

I didn't expect him to answer me, but he did. 'I've really no idea. If Mrs. Galecci wishes to part with them, naturally I'll offer to take them off her hands — at a reasonable price.'

'Thanks. That's all I wanted to know.'

I turned back to Dawn and at that moment, the street door opened. The bell chimed again and three guys walked in. They were all big men. I didn't recognize any of them but I knew they meant trouble. I pushed away from the counter but I wasn't quick enough. For all their size, those bruisers were quick on their feet.

I just glimpsed something in the first guy's right hand as he hit me on the side of the head. Dawn yelled once. Then everything went black and quiet as I dived head first into a sea of blackness that had no bottom.

* * *

The room was small and made even smaller by the number of people packed into it. Cigarette smoke drifted lazily in the air and there was a peculiar rocking motion that I put down to having just regained consciousness. It wasn't Tefler's shop but someplace else.

I pushed myself up groggily onto my elbows, trying to figure out where I was, how I had got there, and how long I had been out. Slowly, my vision adjusted. The first thing I saw was Dawn slumped in the other chair. The second thing that hit me was that the odd rocking motion had nothing to do with my physical condition. The room really was swaying gently from side to side.

I figured out then where we'd been taken. Out to one of the pleasure yachts moored offshore. Most of these were owned by the various bosses of the Organization, and the police normally turned a blind eye to any gambling and the like which went on aboard them.

I turned my head slowly, wincing as something like a white-hot knife sliced through my skull. I could see that Dawn was fully awake and guessed she hadn't been sapped like I had.

A dark shadow drifted in front of my vision and a voice said, 'Guess you've finally decided to join us, Merak.'

I squinted up at the face as it slowly swam into focus. It was one I'd seen someplace before. Danny Delano, hoodlum and hitman. As far as I knew, he'd never worked for Galecci or Rizzio. That set me wondering. Tefler was clearly in league with the mob, or he had some information they didn't want to get out.

Another voice from somewhere on the other side of the cabin said, 'It's unfortunate you can't do exactly as you're told. All of this unpleasantness could have been avoided if you'd just done as I asked you.'

It was Gloria Galecci. I'd have recognized that sultry voice anywhere.

She was leaning against the polished

woodwork, smiling across at me, but it wasn't a nice smile. Rather it was like that of a tigress eyeing up its lunch.

I licked my lips and stared up at Delano. 'I suppose we're going to get to know why we've been brought here. Somehow, I don't think it's for a holiday.'

'Too damned right it isn't. You've been pushing your nose into too many things that don't concern you. You've been officially put off the case but you still persist in going around asking awkward questions.'

'Like I said, I'm just trying to earn the thousand dollars Carlos gave me.'

Delano's hand moved and a fist like a block of concrete smashed me on the side of the head.

Through the tears that threatened to blind me, I saw Dawn start up from the chair. She only got halfway to her feet when Gloria swung an arm and knocked her back again.

I leaned my head back, sucking air into my lungs. I knew this was the tightest spot I'd ever been in. These guys were playing for keeps. I didn't know what it was they figured I'd stumbled on but knowing how they operated, they'd try a little friendly persuasion at first and if that didn't work, they would just tie a few weights around our legs and drop us overboard someplace where the fish would be the only ones to find us.

With an effort, I cleared my vision and scanned the cabin, marking the position of the only exit to the deck and every person in it. Two guys stood in the background, taking very little interest in the proceedings. Gloria stood at the back of Dawn's chair while Delano, who seemed to be running the show, leaned nonchalantly against the table. There was a gun showing in his waistband. It was mine.

The cabin was dimly lit with only a solitary hurricane lamp suspended from the middle of the ceiling. There were two circular windows, one on each side, and through them I saw that it was already getting dark.

'You seem to have taken a sudden unhealthy interest in Tefler,' Delano said. He was smiling now, showing perfect white teeth. 'Just what is it about him that interests you so much?'

I shrugged slightly. 'Nothing important. I'm interested in Galecci's collection, that's all. Figured I might buy one of them, just as a momento, you know, for old time's sake. I rather liked him. He was a crook but he always played straight with me.'

Delano threw back his head and uttered a hearty laugh. 'You're lying through your teeth, Merak. And I don't like it. You couldn't afford to buy anything that belonged to Galecci. Even one of those clocks would set you back more than you earn in ten years.'

He leaned forward and pushed his face up to mine. 'We've no time for stalling. You're going to tell us everything we want to know and we can do it the easy way — or the hard way. It's entirely up to you.'

'If I knew what it is you want to know, maybe I'd tell you,' I said, speaking as coolly as I could. 'But even if I did, we'd still both end up at the bottom of the sea. You can't afford to let us go now.'

'Why should we want to kill you?' Gloria spoke this time. 'You can do nothing to hurt any of us. All we want is information.'

'You know, this is what I like about my job,' I replied. 'Everybody gets to know everybody else. You knowing Delano here, for example. From what I know, he's always been on the opposite side to Carlos. Now you're acting like old buddies. I wonder if Sam knows anything about this?'

Her face changed abruptly. From the sharp glitter in her baby-blue eyes that matched the dress she wore, I knew I'd said the wrong thing.

'I think you'd better be taught that it doesn't do to poke into things you've been told to leave alone. You've been advised to drop this case but it seems you're not the kind to take advice.'

She straightened up to her full majestic height and stared hard at Delano. 'Somehow, I don't think you're going to get anything of value out of him. But there is another way.'

'I can make him talk,' Delano insisted.

'No. Even if you did, we couldn't be sure he's telling the truth. But if I were to rough up his girlfriend a little, that should loosen his tongue.'

'You lay a finger on Dawn and I'll — '

'You're not in a position to do anything,' Gloria snapped. There was a look of malicious anticipation on her face now.

Reaching forward, she grabbed Dawn by the shoulders and hauled her roughly out of the chair. Twisting one arm behind her back, she propelled Dawn towards a door that led into another cabin. Thrusting it open with her free hand, she shoved Dawn through, following her, and slamming the door behind her.

Tensing myself, I stared at the gun in Delano's belt. He wasn't looking at me. Neither were the other two guys across the cabin. They were all staring at the closed door, running their tongues around their lips. I had heard about some of Delano's work among the mobs. It was work that was always done properly and with the least amount of fuss.

He was standing only a couple of feet

from where I sat in the chair but I knew my chances of snatching that gun and using it were so slim as to be non-existent.

Noises came from inside the closed room. I thought I made out a muffled scream and then silence. Gritting my teeth, I could only sit there and listen, picturing to myself what was happening in there. I'd seen Gloria in action with that weight in her gym. I doubted if there was a man in that cabin who would have stood a chance against her in a hand-to-hand fight.

A thud sounded. It was like the noise made by a body hitting a wall. I knew I had to do something to help Dawn. Sitting there and knowing what was happening to her at that moment was pure hell. But I'd have had a slug in me before I could take a couple of steps —

Then the door to the room opened slowly. I pushed myself forward, ready to make a grab for the gun. If it was the last thing I did, I meant to put a bullet into Gloria.

A figure stepped into the cabin, a limp

body draped over her shoulders, arms hanging limply on either side.

Several seconds passed before I realized it was Dawn standing there.

Somehow, I screwed my eyes back into their sockets. There were a couple of seconds when nobody moved. It was as if time had been frozen into a block of ice.

Then Dawn suddenly twisted sharply from the waist and threw Gloria's unconscious body straight at the two guys standing near the exit. I moved fast. Before Delano could turn, or recover from the shock, I'd grabbed the gun from his waistband.

My first shot slammed into Delano's shoulder as he made a lunge for me.

The second took out the hurricane lamp swinging lazily from the ceiling. I had Dawn by the arm and was hustling her towards the stairs leading up to the deck while the glass from the lamp was still falling onto the table.

Kicking the nearer guy in the groin as he tried to get to his feet, I pushed Dawn up the stairs. A quick glance over the rail told me that dry land was about two hundred yards from the yacht. Behind us, confused shouting came from inside the cabin. Delano was yelling orders in a high-pitched, strangled voice. There was the sound of heavy steps on the stairs.

Thrusting the gun into its holster, I pushed Dawn towards the rail.

'Think you can make it to shore?' I yelled.

She gave a quick nod. Together, we went over the rail. We hit the water simultaneously, dived under, swimming strongly away from the vessel.

When I came up for air, I heard something crack sharply behind us and a slug hit the water a couple of feet from me. More shots came but in the darkness, they were firing blind. I knew it would be only a matter of minutes before they got a light up onto the deck. These yachts often had a searchlight available to check on any boats coming out to them. Also, somebody would soon get the idea of launching a small boat after us.

It was a long haul but finally we dragged ourselves up onto a low break-water, coughing water out of our lungs.

Eventually, the coughing subsided and my heart went back into its rightful place. I stared across at Dawn.

'How the hell did you manage to get the better of that dame?' I asked. 'I've seen her in action. She's twice as strong as any ox.'

Somehow, she managed a smile. 'My Daddy always wanted a son. When I came along, he decided there might come a time when I'd have to take care of myself. So he taught me some moves which might come in useful.' She made a swift, downward chopping motion with her stiffened right hand. 'Like he always told me, the bigger they come, the harder they fall.'

I grinned even though it hurt my face where Delano had slugged me. 'I'll have to remember that in case I come up against her again.'

'After what happened there, I don't think that will be too long,' Dawn said gravely. 'I reckon they want us both dead. For some reason, they seem to think you know a lot more than you do.'

'And right now, I wish I knew what it

is.' I stood up, swayed a little as everything started a carousel ride around me.

Dawn caught my arm. 'You need to get your head seen to,' she said. 'Not just what's inside it, but that's a nasty wound you have.'

'I'll be okay in a couple of minutes.' I checked the luminous dial of my watch. It was a little after eight. 'There are still a couple of things I have to do.'

'Won't they wait until tomorrow, Johnny?'

I shook my head. The world spun a little faster, then settled down. 'By tomorrow it may be too late.'

She uttered a sigh of exasperation. 'All right. Where are we going this time?'

'Back to the place where we were so rudely interrupted. I've got some unfinished business there and this time Tefler is going to talk whether he likes it or not.'

'You're a goddamned fool. That's exactly what they'll expect you to do. They'll be waiting for you and this time you may not get out alive.'

'That's a chance I'll have to take, I

guess.' I turned my head very slowly in case the merry-go-round started up again. 'First, we'll have to find out just where we are.'

We started walking. There was nobody about. The narrow streets were as empty as my stomach was feeling at that moment. However, the fresh air helped.

Within five minutes I was feeling in better shape. I felt like a drowned rat with my sodden clothing sticking to my limbs and although Dawn looked great with her dress clinging tightly to her curves, I knew we had to steer clear of any crowds or folk might start asking funny questions.

A narrow alley led onto a sign that said Twenty-First Street and I now had a good idea where we were. Seemingly, those hoods hadn't taken us too far from where they'd picked us up. We ploughed our way over to Appleton Street and then angled onto Main without meeting a single soul and with only a handful of cars passing us.

Tefler's shop stood almost midway along Main and even from a distance of a hundred yards I could see the Merc was still there at the kerb where I'd parked it. Evidently our captors had been certain we'd never be coming back to claim it.

There was a light in the window of Tefler's shop. A dim light but from what I'd seen earlier, that guy preferred to live in almost constant gloom.

'Be careful,' Dawn cautioned as we sidled up to it. 'Even if those crooks on that yacht haven't got here already, there are such things as telephones.'

I gave the front of the place a thorough once-over. There was no sign of anyone in the street. If anyone were watching the shop, they'd probably be some distance away using high-powered binoculars.

Between the shop and the adjacent building was a narrow passage that didn't even merit the designation of an alley. I motioned Dawn towards it with my hand, taking out the .38 with the other. After five minutes that seemed like five hours, I decided the passage was deserted. I couldn't be absolutely certain but there seemed no sense in just standing there like the Statue of Liberty.

'Let's go,' I said in a whisper. Making no noise, we edged along the passage. At the end was an open space littered with piles of rubbish.

Something black scurried out of sight at our approach. I guess it wasn't often the rodent population were disturbed by any intruders.

There were a couple of windows at the rear of Tefler's place. I'd expected them to be barred just in case some slippery-fingered thief took an urge to heist some of the jewelry he had stashed inside. But there was nothing like that. Even the woodwork around the glass looked rotten.

All in all, it seemed just a little too inviting, too easy. Reaching up, I ran my fingers along the wall on either side of the nearer window. It was just as I'd figured. There was a wire running across the brick to somewhere above our heads. Try to force the window and doubtless an alarm would sound somewhere inside and also at police headquarters. Evidently Tefler was taking no chances with his merchandise falling into the wrong hands.

Taking out my penknife, I prayed that

whoever had rigged up this alarm system was no smarter than I was and cut the wire. Nothing happened. No bells started ringing inside the building. It was the work of a couple of minutes to work the glass free of its rotten surrounds and place the pane carefully against the wall.

'You can wait outside if you want to,' I said as Dawn sidled up beside me. 'It's just possible there's a welcoming committee inside.'

Dawn looked around the overgrown dump. I guess she knew she'd have rats for company if she stayed. 'I'll come with you.' Her voice trembled just a little.

Somehow, I pulled myself through the opening, twisted, and landed softly on my feet. Reaching down, I gave Dawn a helping hand.

Everything was quiet, too quiet. Judging by the light we'd seen, Tefler should have been somewhere around but like the rats, he wasn't making much noise. Feeling our way forward, we reached the far corner of the room. My outstretched fingers encountered a door and there was a narrow sliver of yellow light showing around one edge.

I tried the doorknob, twisting it slowly. It wasn't locked. Very slowly, I pulled it open and peered through the gap. It was the door leading into the rear of the front shop. I could see the counter right in front of me, the ghostly shapes of the clocks still making their eternal ticking. There was no sign of Tefler.

Taking a chance, I stepped through. There was something wrong. I could smell it. A little voice was chattering away inside my head, screaming at me to go back the way I'd come and get the hell out of the vicinity. Stupidly, I ignored it, told it to lie down and keep quiet.

I walked along the back of the counter and into the main area of the shop.

I'd been mistaken. Tefler was still there but he wasn't taking any interest in his shop. He was lying on the floor in front of the counter and there was a knife sticking out of the middle of his back.

I heard Dawn's sharp intake of breath as she stopped and peered over my shoulder.

'It's Tefler, isn't it?' she gasped. 'Is he dead?'

'Couldn't be more dead,' I said. 'He can't have been dead long. The body's still warm.'

'But why — ?'

I straightened and it was right at that moment that there was another sound superimposed upon the endless ticking of those damned clocks.

It was a police siren somewhere in the street outside.

The next second, the patrol car slid to a screeching halt outside the shop. Three guys got out and ran for the door. One of them smashed it in with his shoulder and then they were inside, covering Dawn and I with their guns.

Two of them looked like regular patrol officers.

The third was Lieutenant Donovan.

4

Donovan walked towards the body without looking in my direction. There was a nasty look in his eye and I could see he was enjoying every minute of this. He must have figured that Tefler was already dead but he went down on one knee and made an elaborate charade of feeling for the pulse. Then he peered closely at the knife handle in the old guy's back before straightening up.

'I think you'll find that knife is the identical twin to the one which killed Galecci,' I said.

In the circumstances it wasn't the right thing to say but I wanted to break the ice somehow.

'Right now, I'm not interested in the knife, Merak,' he said acidly. 'It looks to me as though you're both in a whole heap of trouble. I reckon you'll have a lot of explaining to do down at the precinct. Found kneeling over the body after breaking into the place. Looks real bad to me.'

'Who says we broke in?' Dawn demanded heatedly.

Donovan spun on her as if he was on wheels, his face twisted. 'I say so. That front door was locked when we arrived and unless you came in and locked it after you, he certainly didn't get up off the floor to pick it after he'd been knifed.'

He jerked a thumb towards one of the cops standing near the street door.

'Check the rear of this place. I think you'll find some signs of forced entry.'

'I can save you the trouble,' I said. 'That's the way we got in. I had to check on Tefler and I also wanted to ask him a few questions.'

'Did you now? So instead of coming to the street door like any ordinary person would and ringing the bell, you decided to break in and surprise him. Is that how it was?' Donovan bared his teeth in a malicious grin. 'I reckon you'll have to think up a better story than that.'

'Don't try to pin this murder on us, Donovan,' I said harshly. 'I've got a witness this time as to what's happened tonight.'

Donovan's stony glance switched to Dawn. His grin widened. 'Somehow, I doubt if the D.A. or a jury will be inclined to accept that evidence. It's more likely I'll be charging her with complicity to murder.'

'Like hell she will. Even you're not so stupid as to seriously think that. Tefler was killed about an hour ago. Even I can tell that. The body's still warm and rigor is just beginning to set in. At that time, we were both being held prisoner on one of the yachts out there. You know, the one's the mobs use for their entertainment. Or do you seriously think we make a habit of walking the streets at night soaking wet? If you want my opinion, which you probably don't, this is the work of either Sam Rizzio or Danny Delano.'

Donovan's brows went up so far they almost disappeared under his hat.

'Now why should either of them want him out of the way? He was no threat to them.'

I could see that Donovan was listening

to me but his eyes told me he was thinking other thoughts.

'Delano and a couple of his bruisers were on that yacht. Maybe they'd guessed I'd come to talk with Tefler just after the funeral and I'm damn sure he knew a lot more about the identity of Galecci's killer than he was saying. If they figured he was likely to spill something to me once I put the heat on, they'd want him out of the way — permanently.'

'Then you admit you came here to put the squeeze on Tefler?'

'We tailed him after the funeral. Before that, I'd no idea who he was. But he was a frightened man although he told us very little before clamming up. But Rizzio and Delano weren't to know that. They couldn't afford to take the chance of him squealing. While we were talking, some of their boys came into the shop and one of them sapped me. The next thing I knew, I was out there on the water. Tefler was alive when I got knocked out.'

Donovan gave a long, hard look at my clothes, then Dawn's. I guess he figured there had to be a little truth in what I was saying. But he still wasn't totally convinced.

'You haven't explained why you broke into the place.'

'Isn't it obvious? Once we got away from that yacht, their first guess would be that we'd head for here. If I hadn't been certain that Tefler knew something important before then, the fact they wanted us dead, now made me doubly certain. They'd get a message ashore and by the time we got here, they'd have a welcoming committee waiting just inside that door. I'm not such a fool as to walk into an ambush with my eyes shut.'

Donovan still shook his head. I could see he was desperate to pin this rap on me but now he wasn't sure he could make it stick. His gaze was going over my face, pore by pore, trying to read into it something that wasn't there.

'You reckon you're so goddamned smart, Merak,' he muttered finally. 'But you'd better know I don't believe half of what you've said. I can still hold you for breaking and entering. That could put you away for a while at least.'

'But you won't.'

'Don't tempt me,' he said threateningly. 'I'm beginning to lose my patience where you're concerned. Maybe if you were locked away for a time, I might — '

'You might go back to being the regular nice guy you used to be,' I interrupted.

'Very funny.' He closed his mouth slowly.

'Just as a matter of interest, how did you know about Tefler?' I asked.

'No mystery about that. We got a tip-off there was some kind of trouble here.'

'And did this caller give a name?' I knew the answer to that question before I asked it. Maybe my guess about somebody with binoculars watching from further along the street hadn't been too wide of the mark, after all. They'd seen Dawn and I near the shop and put in the call. Maybe Rizzio or Delano, whoever it was now calling the shots, reckoned that having us killed could create plenty of trouble for them. It would be much simpler having us framed for Tefler's murder.

'So what happens now, Lieutenant?' I

asked. 'Are you going to arrest us for murder?'

Donovan looked down at the body, then back to me. I could see he was thinking deep thoughts, turning over all of the possibilities in his mind before replying.

Finally, he said, 'Get the hell out of here, Merak, before I change my mind.' The words must have burned his mouth like acid. 'You won't be going anywhere and I can have you picked up anytime. Besides, I think you're in enough trouble with Rizzio and Delano. Somehow, I don't think your lives are worth a plugged nickel right now. One or other of them might save me the trouble.'

I knew he was right. Somehow, Tefler had known too much — and now he'd paid the price for it.

Taking Dawn's arm, I led her outside and along to the car. We were both shivering. The night air was cold, biting through our wet clothing. But the chill went deeper than that. Donovan hadn't meant it to be funny when he'd hinted that we could both be on Rizzio's or

Delano's hit list. And I also had the feeling that Gloria Galecci was in on the act somewhere. What I couldn't figure was why she was in with Delano. As far as I knew, he and Galecci were sworn enemies. There'd been a feud not so long since over some disputed territory. Even with Galecci gone, why should Gloria join up with him — unless it was to get Rizzio out of the way.

'It's time we got out of these wet clothes,' Dawn said as I turned the car and drove back along Main. 'Better go back to my place.'

'I don't have any spare clothes there,' I said.

'Those you have on will dry overnight in front of the fire.' She gave me the lovely smile with a world of meaning in it.

We got to Dawn's place a quarter of an hour later. There was no sign of anyone suspicious hanging around as we went in.

After she had locked the door and slipped the bolt into place, we went through into the lounge where she turned on the electric fire. I began to feel warm all over.

'You'd better get out of those wet things right now,' she said. 'Help yourself to a drink.'

I poured myself a Scotch, set the glass on the table and peeled off my jacket while she went into the other room. When she came back she was wearing a deep red dressing gown and I guessed nothing else.

Sipping my drink, I sat back and closed my eyes. It had been a hectic day.

Dawn had a worried expression on her face as she poured herself a drink. She held out one hand towards the fire. 'What do you think, Johnny?' she asked. 'Donovan wasn't kidding when he said Rizzio or Delano would take care of us.'

'No, he wasn't. I'm beginning to think I was wrong getting involved in this case. Not only is it way out of my league but it's put you in danger too.'

'Don't worry on my account, Johnny. I can take care of myself. We're in this together now.'

I drank the other half of my drink and wished I felt as confident as she was trying to be.

'Someone knew we were tailing Tefler,' I said, speaking my thoughts out aloud. 'Somebody who then tipped off Delano. That's what I don't get. Why him? If they were scared I'd get the little guy to talk about Galecci's murder, why wasn't Rizzio the one involved?'

'Don't forget Mrs. Galecci.'

I nodded. 'Another puzzle. She's clearly well in with Delano. The only thing I can think of is that she's trying to get him to kill Rizzio and leave the field clear for her to take over.'

Dawn sighed. 'If you're right there could soon be a full-scale gang war about to break out and unless you're lucky, you could be right in the middle of it because it seems to me that somebody believes you know who killed Galecci — and how.' She glanced at me sideways. 'Do you?'

'I haven't the faintest idea,' I told her. 'But whoever did it, he's damned clever.'

'Or she,' Dawn corrected.

I shook my head. 'Somehow I doubt if Gloria has the brains to work out a killing like that.'

Dawn yawned. 'Leave it until tomorrow. You might see things clearer then.'

Getting up, she went back into the bedroom and came out with a bathrobe. 'Get out of the rest of those wet things and put this on,' she said quietly.

I did as she said and then followed her. There was only a single dim light in the room and no sound apart from the dull roar of the city traffic in the distance.

Dawn let her robe drop, then slid into the bed, holding the sheet back on the other side. I could just make out that faint smile on her lips. 'You're not going to argue with me, are you?' she said softly.

'I never argue with a woman who can knock Gloria Galecci cold and then carry her out of the room,' I said, moving in beside her.

★　★　★

It was already light when I woke the next morning. I sat up and for a few moments, tried to figure out where I was. Then it all came back to me. There was no sign of Dawn and my clothes were draped carefully over the back of the chair near the bed.

I dressed quickly and went through into the parlor. There was the smell of bacon and eggs cooking in the kitchen. Dawn came in a couple of minutes later and laid the heaped plates on the small table.

'I'll wager this is the first real meal you've eaten for days,' she said, seating herself opposite me.

'You should know that in this job you often have to eat on the hoof,' I said, picking up the knife and fork. The breakfast tasted as delicious as it looked and I ate ravenously.

Dawn brought the coffee after we had finished. It burned my throat but it gave the perfect ending to the meal. Sitting back, I lit a cigarette and offered her one.

Blowing the smoke into the air, I felt more able to face the world again.

I still had those little mice scampering around inside my head and none of them were making any sense.

Dawn finished her coffee and said, 'I almost forgot. I mentioned before that I'd managed to get a little information for you on Rizzio and Mrs. Galecci. A friend of mine knows the woman who does some of the cleaning at the Galecci place. It seems there's no love lost between those two. Even when Galecci was alive there were frequent rows. I got the impression Rizzio had the feeling she was out to oust him even then.'

'So all we've got is that now Galecci is dead, she means to make use of that will to push him out altogether.'

'You think she has the guts to run an organization like that?' Dawn placed her cup carefully on the table and stubbed out her cigarette.

'I'd say she's got the guts all right. But I doubt whether any of those hoods will take orders from a woman. Rizzio is a natural as far as that's concerned. Maybe that's why she's suddenly so close to Delano. She's relying on him to help her take over.'

It was nice to reach some conclusion that made sense but I still wasn't sure it was the right one.

'I reckon it's time I found out a little

more of what's happening between Rizzio and Gloria and there's only one place I can find it.'

'Where's that?'

'Right at the top,' I said harshly. 'Somehow, I have to talk to Rizzio. Maybe if he's not aware of this liaison between Gloria and Delano he might be grateful enough for the information to give me some in return.'

'And maybe he'll shoot you on sight.' Dawn exclaimed.

'I guess that's a risk I'll have to take. At the moment, I seem to be getting nowhere fast.'

Dawn spread her hands resignedly. 'If you've made up your mind, there's nothing I can do to stop you but I still think that blow on your head has affected your reason.'

5

I knew I'd be asking for trouble if I just presented myself at the gates of the Galecci place and asked to come in. With a man like Rizzio it was wiser to put in a telephone call and make a polite request.

Back at my office, I checked the number and then dialed, hoping I didn't get Gloria on the line. That would have made things very difficult.

Some guy answered. It wasn't Rizzio.

'I'd like to speak to Sam Rizzio,' I said, using his first name in the hope that it might get me a better reception.

'Who wants to speak to him?' The voice told me this had better be good or the line would go dead within a couple of seconds.

'If he's in, tell him that Johnny Merak wants to see him on *important* business.' I deliberately stressed the 'important'.

A pause, then, 'Hold the line.'

I waited.

Then, 'That you, Merak?' This time it was Rizzio's voice and he sounded impatient. 'I thought you'd been told to drop this case.'

'Not exactly,' I said. 'In fact, I've been told to stay on it.'

'The hell you have!' He was snarling the words. If he'd been a wolf and there was a full moon, he'd have been baying at it. 'Who's told you that?'

'I'm afraid that this time, I must respect my client's confidentiality.' I replied. 'Let's just say he lives way out in the country and he has a personal interest in Galecci's death.'

There was a pause nearly long enough to eat a three-course meal. When he spoke again, there was a complete change in his manner. I knew he'd figured out who I was talking about.

'I think you'd better come over right away,' he said. 'And it had better be important.'

'It is,' I said, and rang off. I could picture him staring down at the receiver in his hand and wondering how the hell I'd got in with Manzelli.

Half an hour later, I parked the car in exactly the same place as on the last occasion when Rizzio had asked me to come over. It looked like the same two guys at the gate but after a while they all looked the same to me. This time, however, they didn't even bother to ask my name. They still took away my .38 from me but this was just a formality.

I walked up the drive and on this occasion, Rizzio was there, waiting at the door.

'All right, Merak,' he said in a voice that would have frozen a furnace. 'What is it you wish to see me about? I gather it has something to do with Carlos' death.'

Without giving me a chance to reply, he turned and led the way inside. He took me into the big room I'd seen before and motioned to the chair facing the desk.

Seating himself in the other chair, he stared directly at me. 'Well? Is it something to do with Carlos?'

'Not exactly.' I came straight to the point. 'Do you happen to know anything about this will Galecci made out just before he was killed?'

A look of genuine surprise flitted across his face. He sat very still, as if listening for something. Then he shook his head. 'No. And just what do you know about it?'

'Only this. That Carlos left everything to Gloria, including all of the business he'd built up in LA. Now if that's true, I'd say it puts you in a very awkward position.'

Rizzio got quickly to his feet. For a moment, I thought he was going to lean across the desk and put one on my jaw. Instead, he crossed to a small cabinet and took out a bottle and two glasses.

'I don't particularly like you, Merak,' he said thinly. 'But you've got an honest face and I can't think of any reason why you should be lying.' He filled the glasses and pushed one across to me. It slid smoothly across the polished desk without spilling a drop.

'I'm not lying and somehow, call it a hunch if you like, I don't think you killed Carlos. In fact, I don't even think you had anything to do with it, although you did have a pretty strong motive.'

He smiled at that. It must have been

the first time he'd smiled in years. He should have had a photograph taken of it as a momento for future years.

'So do you have any ideas on who did murder him?'

'I'm following up some leads,' I said. 'But there's nothing definite so far. If I do come across anything, you'll be the first to know — after my new client, of course.'

'Of course.' He downed his drink and poured himself another. I still nursed half of mine.

'One other thing I reckon you ought to know. Gloria seems to be on more than just talking terms with Danny Delano.'

That shook him. His face whitened perceptibly under the playboy tan. 'Are you sure of that?'

'Let's just say that a couple of Delano's thugs sapped me yesterday and took me out to one of those luxury yachts. Gloria was there and they seemed real pally.'

'The lying, cheating little bitch!' Rizzio's teeth were clamped together so tightly I thought they'd crack under the strain. 'If you can provide me with proof that she had a hand in murdering Carlos, I'll take care of her — for good.'

'Personally, I can't see her having the know-how to plan a perfect murder like that.'

'Then who?'

'Delano maybe. But somehow, that doesn't fit either. I've got a gut feeling there's someone else, someone in the shadows that we haven't thought of yet.'

Rizzio looked thoughtful as he sipped his second drink. Finally, he leaned back, one hand still around his glass. 'You've been very helpful, Merak,' he said genially. 'I won't forget it. To be quite honest, I never thought Gloria wanted anything to do with the Organization. I figured she'd be a very rich woman once she got her hands on Carlos' money and she'd go to live somewhere in style, California perhaps, maybe get her claws into some other rich guy.'

'That's the way it usually goes,' I agreed. 'But if she goes ahead with this scheme of hers, how do you figure the rest of the boys will take to it? You reckon they'll throw in their lot with you — or with her?'

'They'll throw in with me.' Rizzio sounded confident but I knew he was thinking fast. This news had spooked him and he wasn't sure what to do about it. But I'd done what I'd set out to do; planted the seeds of doubt in his mind and, with a bit of luck, taken some of the heat off Dawn and myself.

Right now, Rizzio was figuring out the best way to get rid of Gloria. She, for her part, would be doing the same where he was concerned.

I butted in on his thoughts. 'There are a couple of things you might do for me,' I said.

He brought his eyes round to look directly at me. 'Like I said, your information has been very helpful. What can I do for you?'

'That knife which killed Galecci. I presume you had a good look at it. Have you ever seen any others exactly the same?'

He shook his head. 'Not that I can

recollect. Why? Is it important?'

'I think it is. You see, an identical knife was used to kill Anton Tefler last night. To me, that suggests that the same person killed both men.'

Rizzio nodded slowly, thoughtfully. 'I heard about Tefler. If you're asking me if I know who might have killed him, the answer's — no. As far as I know, he had no enemies.'

'My guess is that he knew too much.'

'About Carlos' death?'

'That's right.'

'That seems hard to believe. I don't know what reason you have for thinking that, but he was only an agent for Carlos. He scoured the world for clocks for his collection and — '

'Any possibility that some of those antiques might have been obtained by other than strictly legitimate means?'

Rizzio spread his hands. 'That's possible. Carlos had the dough to get anything he wanted. Who's to say how Tefler obtained them?'

I had a funny thought at that moment. 'You don't think someone may have found out about this and was black-mailing the little guy?'

'You're snatching at straws, Merak. You'll have to do better than that if you're to crack this case.'

'Yeah, you're probably right.' I half rose to my feet, then stopped and looked down at him. 'Just one other thing. How well do you know Donovan?'

He smiled the faintest smile in the world and shook his head. 'I hardly know the man at all. I know he's a lieutenant in Homicide and he's been assigned to this case. There's not much more I can tell you.'

'Did Galecci know him any better? I mean, were there any occasions when Donovan was invited here?'

Something sparked at the back of Rizzio's eyes. 'What exactly do you mean by that?'

I decided to push my luck in spite of the hard expression on Rizzio's face. 'Let's say we all know who really pulls the strings in LA, even where the police department is concerned. There are crooked cops in every force. I've no doubt that our mutual friend out in the country funds millions of dollars getting the right people elected into nearly every public office.'

'And you're suggesting that Galecci had Donovan in his pocket?'

'It's possible.'

'If he did, he kept it to himself. Now if there's nothing else you wish to discuss — '

'Not a thing,' I said. 'But as I told you earlier — watch your back. Galecci and Tefler forgot to do that and they both paid the price.'

'Thanks for the warning.' The way he said it made it sound genuine. He accompanied me to the door.

'Just one more thing,' I said as I prepared to leave.

He gave me a funny look. 'It seems to me you've got a lot of just one more things on your mind, Merak.'

'That's the way it is in my business.'

'All right. I guess I owe you one. What is it this time?'

'If you've got any pull with somebody high up in Homicide, I'd like to get

Donovan off my back for a while. At the moment, he's keen to pin Tefler's murder on me.'

Rizzio smiled bleakly. 'Now why should I do that, even if I could?'

'For two reasons, I guess. Because I think you want to get to the bottom of this affair as much as I do.'

'And the other reason?'

I looked him straight in the eye. 'Because, right now, I figure you need all the friends you can get.'

He said nothing to that but I knew he was thinking on his feet, going over everything I'd said. He was no fool. With the information I'd fed him, he'd have Gloria watched like a hawk and if he wanted to reduce the odds, there'd be a hit out on Delano before I reached the gates.

I drove back to the office. As soon as I opened the door I sensed trouble.

Dawn was there — and Donovan. He was standing in front of the desk tapping the top with his fingers. He had that look on his face that boded no good for anyone who got in his way.

'I told the Lieutenant you'd be back soon, Johnny,' Dawn said. She sounded worried.

'All right, I'm back.' I sat down in my chair and placed my hat carefully on the desk. Pulling out a pack of cigarettes from the drawer, I lit one and watched the smoke spiral lazily towards the ceiling. 'I take it this isn't a social call, Lieutenant.'

'Too damned right, it isn't.' Donovan leaned forward over the desk, glaring at me. 'I still have a lot of questions to ask and you'd better answer them or I'm taking you down to the precinct and you'll answer them there.'

'Here will be fine.'

'Don't try to sideslip me, Merak. I listened to that story you spun me last night and then went over it with the D.A. He doesn't believe much of it either. Reckons I've got enough to bring you in on suspicion of murder.'

'Does he now? You've got no evidence at all and you know it.'

'I've got plenty!' he snapped. 'A witness who's prepared to swear he saw you and your assistant prowling around that shop not more than ten minutes before we arrived on the scene.'

'We've already told you that,' I said, leaning back in the chair. 'But that was almost an hour after Tefler was stabbed.'

'We don't know that for sure until an autopsy has been carried out.'

'And the knife,' I pointed out. 'Exactly the same as that which killed Galecci. Makes you think, doesn't it? Two identical knives, both men stabbed in the back. I'd say it was the same person killed both. And, somehow, I doubt if you could place me at Galecci's when he was murdered.'

'I don't have to. Placing you at the scene of the second murder is good enough for me and — '

He broke off sharply as the phone on my desk shrilled loudly. I picked it up. I thought it might be Rizzio. But it wasn't. It was the D.A. asking if Donovan was there.

I handed the phone to him. 'It's for you,' I said. 'The D.A.'

I could just hear the D.A.'s voice on the other end of the line and even though I couldn't make out the words, it made

114

Donovan's face go even redder than usual. Whatever it was, he seemed to be pretty sharp with him. Donovan said little beyond a couple of 'buts' and 'yes sirs' before replacing the phone in its cradle and straightening up. There was a pained look on his face.

'Something wrong, Lieutenant?' I asked sweetly.

'Seems the two of you are off the hook,' he replied through tightly clenched teeth. 'Some nosy fisherman heard shots being fired on one of the yachts last night around the time Tefler must have been murdered. Says he saw two people swimming towards the quay, a man and a woman. Like a good citizen he reported it to the police this morning.'

With what was supposed to be an apologetic grimace, he added, 'I reckon there can't have been two couples running around in wet clothes in that part of town.'

'God bless the decent citizens of LA,' I remarked. 'Then I reckon you won't have any further questions for us, Lieutenant.'

'No. But I'm still warning you to keep

your nose out of police business.'

He looked as though he could chew on an iron bar and spit out nails. 'I'm not through with you yet.'

He went out, closing the door loudly behind him.

I watched him go. Grinning at Dawn, I said, 'Now there goes a very unhappy man.'

Dawn walked over and leaned against the side of the desk, eyeing me curiously. 'Now why do I get the feeling that you knew something like this was going to happen? You didn't seem too worried when he threatened to take us in on a murder charge.'

'Let's just say that my little talk with Sam Rizzio paid off dividends sooner than I expected.'

I wasn't sure whether Rizzio had got onto the D.A. off his own bat, or whether Manzelli had heard what had happened and he had put the screws on the D.A. Either way, it had eased the pressure from Donovan. Right now, there was one big question uppermost in my mind. Gloria and Danny Delano. Two pieces of the jigsaw on opposite sides of the picture, yet now together. Just how close were they? Clearly, Gloria was using Delano to further her plans for taking over complete control of her late husband's empire.

I needed to know how close this unholy union was and what she intended to do. I wasn't likely to get any information from either of them but I had other sources, a few of which might be persuaded to talk to me.

'What are you figuring on doing now, Johnny?' Dawn asked. 'I can tell by your face you've got something in mind.'

'That's right,' I said. 'I need to check on Delano and his relationship with Gloria Galecci. There are a few people I might ask.'

'Petty crooks and hoodlums.'

'Are there any other kind?'

Dawn's face was hard. 'One of these days they're going to fish you out of the water or find you lying face down in some back alley. You know that, don't you?'

I shrugged. 'This isn't my usual case, Dawn. I've just been drawn into it. I'm more used to finding errant husbands who've skipped town without paying their alimony. Or husbands who want photographs and hotel receipts to show where their wives have been instead of spending the weekend at their mother's.'

'Then why go on with this case? It's not as if you're going to make a fortune out of it.'

'I guess at first it was the challenge of cracking a murder that couldn't possibly have been committed,' I told her truthfully. 'But once I got drawn into it, there was no way of backing out. You don't just give up when there are men like Manzelli giving the orders. That isn't conducive to a long and healthy life.'

'Then go ahead and get yourself killed. See if I care.'

'But you do care.'

She stared hard at me for a minute and I could swear there were tears in her eyes. Then she said hoarsely, 'Yes, I do care, Johnny. You know damned well I do.'

She turned away quickly and pretended to busy herself straightening out the papers on the desk.

'I'll watch my step,' I promised her.

'Then at least tell me where you're going and when you'll be back.'

'Okay, if it makes you feel better. First, I want to have a word with Tefler's neighbors. Somebody may have heard or seen something last night. Then there are a couple of guys who've passed me important information in the past. Maybe they know something I don't.'

She seemed on the point of saying something more as I slammed my hat back onto my head. But when I looked back her lips were pressed tightly together and she wasn't looking at me.

I parked the Merc at the far end of Main Street a quarter of an hour later. Tefler's shop was a murder scene and nobody would be allowed near it without Donovan's say-so. I recalled there was a small tailor's shop adjacent to the jeweler's. Sometimes, these guys worked well into the night if business was good and in a quarter of town like this, very little went on without someone noticing it.

A police car was parked at the kerb immediately in front of Tefler's shop. There was no one in it and I guessed they were all inside, still looking for clues.

The name over the shop window said: *Simon Bergstein, Tailor.* I tried the door. It was locked but after I had knocked twice on the wooden lintel at the side, there came the sound of shuffling footsteps. A key turned in the lock and the door opened about six inches.

'Mister Bergstein?' I said.

'Yes. Who are you? The shop is closed for the day.'

'The name's Merak,' I told him. 'I'm a private detective. I'd like a little information.'

'Information? About what?'

'Can we talk inside?'

Bergstein stared at me for a long minute. There was no doubt he was scared and unsure of me. Then, easing himself back into the shop, he stood on one side, throwing a wary glance in both directions along the street.

'If it's about that terrible affair last night, I know nothing,' he declared, shuffling in front of me along a narrow passage and into the main part of the shop.

It was dim and dusty inside. Suits hung on long metal rails against one wall and there was a big pine table with an ancient sewing machine on it. A couple of long rolls of cloth leaned like drunken hobos in one corner.

I noticed a stairway at one side. 'I guess you live here, over the shop,' I said.

'So?'

I switched the subject. 'Did you know Mister Tefler well?'

He hesitated, then nodded. 'Of course. I knew him for more than twenty years. But I've told all of this to the police officer.'

'Just tell it to me again. I'm sure you want his killer brought to justice just as much as I do. Were you here last night between about seven and nine?'

'I was upstairs listening to the radio.'

'And you neither heard nor saw anything out of the ordinary?'

'That's right.' He was fidgeting nervously with his hands. 'There weren't any gunshots or I would have heard them.'

'But you did hear the police patrol car when it arrived?'

'Oh, sure. They make plenty of noise.'

'And nothing before that?'

He thought that over and I guessed there was something on his mind, maybe something he'd forgotten, or figured too trivial to mention, and it had just come back to him.

'There was another car now that I come to think about it. But that was about an hour before the police came.'

'Did it stop outside Tefler's?'

'No.'

'You're absolutely certain about that?'

'I went to the window. I remember now. It stopped some way up the street. Somebody got out and the car drove off.'

'What type of car was it?' I asked. 'One of those big flashy limousines?'

He shook his head. 'Nothing like that. Something like the police patrol car that came later only there were no lights on it and the man who got out wasn't dressed like an officer.'

I offered him a cigarette, which he took and placed between his lips. His hands were shaking and I lit it for him.

'You're being very helpful, Mister Bergstein,' I said, lighting my own. 'Now one more thing. Did you happen to see where that man who got out of this car went?'

'Sure. He crossed over to the other side of the street. He could have gone into any of the places over there. There aren't many lights here so I couldn't tell.'

Or he could have been waiting in the shadows until he was sure no one was around and then went into Telfer's and killed the old guy, I thought.

'Have you told any of this to the police?' I asked.

'About this other car? No, it only just came into my mind. Why — is it important? I didn't connect it with poor Anton's death.'

'You did right,' I said, stubbing out my cigarette and moving towards the door. 'Most likely, it was nothing. Don't worry about it.'

I went out into the street. The police car was still there in front of Telfer's shop. Someone came out as I turned and walked back to my car. It was no one I knew and I guessed it was one of Donovan's team still going over the place for clues.

I drove downtown to one of the blocks just behind Central Avenue. It was one of those places that had been up since the beginning of the century. It had seen everything from before the roaring twenties to prohibition and the gangster era and still lived to tell the tale. Dingy bars, nightclubs and strip shows, sitting side by side like gray old ladies knitting in front of the guillotine, waiting for the blade to fall.

The gaudy neon lights were mostly dead at this time of day. I sought out a bar called *Davy's* and went inside. Most of the tables were empty but there were several figures lined up along the bar. They had their backs to me, and none of them turned their heads to look to see who had come in.

At the far end were a couple of pool tables with fly-speckled lamps swinging over them. Both were occupied and the click of balls was the only sound in the smoke-filled gloom. A couple of bartenders lazed behind the bar, cigarettes drooping half-forgotten from their lips.

I soon spotted the guy I wanted to talk to. A little runt, his diminutive frame perched on a high stool, legs dangling off the floor. Rusty Morvin, small-time dope pedlar and thief. He looked nothing out of the ordinary but rumor had it that he carried two long-bladed knives, one beneath each armpit, and he could skewer a man thirty yards away with the accuracy and speed of a circus knife-thrower.

The stools on either side of him were vacant and I parked myself on the one to his left.

'Hello, Rusty,' I said genially. 'I figured I might find you here this time of day.'

He didn't turn his head. He was watching me closely through the dusty mirror at the back of the bar. 'What brings you here, Johnny?'

'You,' I said. 'I reckon you've still got your ear to the ground and I just want a little information.'

'About what?'

'First, what have you heard lately about Danny Delano?'

His lips twisted, showing tobacco-stained teeth and he shifted slightly on the stool as though his spine hurt him.

'Believe me, Johnny, I know nothing at all about Delano. He's one guy you steer well clear of if you value your health.'

I fished inside my wallet and took out a couple of ten-dollar bills, holding them in my fist where he could see them.

'I've heard some talk that he's thinking of throwing in his lot with Galecci's widow. You know anything about that?'

His shifty eyes flicked from one end of the bar to the other. None of the other clients on either side of him had moved a muscle. They could have been dummies brought in by the management from the local waxworks to make the place look busy for all the signs of life they showed.

Licking his lips nervously, he muttered, 'Sure, there's been some talk like that. But me — I reckon that's all it is, just talk. Delano may act tough but he wouldn't stand a chance in hell if he went up against Sam Rizzio.'

'That's the way I see it,' I affirmed. I slipped him one of the bills and he looked longingly at the other, like a dog drooling over a bone. He emptied his glass and I signaled to the bartender to bring him another. 'So you don't know anything else about Delano?'

Rusty stared hard at the liquor being poured into his glass, then took it and threw half of it down his throat. He wiped the back of his hand across his mouth. 'I did hear that some guy flew in from Chicago a couple of days ago. Delano's man was at the airport to pick him up. Don't ask me what that adds up to. I keep my nose clear where those boys are concerned.'

Two of the men playing pool finished their game and came over for more drinks and I waited until they'd moved to one of the tables before speaking again.

'Lieutenant Donovan,' I said softly. 'What do you know about him? Do you reckon it's likely he's taking orders from any of the mobs?'

'Donovan?' Rusty looked at me out of the corner of his eye as though I'd just uttered the worst kind of blasphemy. 'What makes you think he's a bent cop?'

'Maybe I'm just being paranoid about him. But he's doing his best to get me off this case I'm working on. If there's nothing funny about him, I'd have reckoned he'd have welcomed any help he could get. Instead, he even tried to frame me over this guy Tefler's murder.'

Rusty shrugged. His gaze flickered once more to the bill in my hand. 'I got no liking for cops but everything I'd heard says that he's a straight guy, or he used to be. One of the best in Homicide.'

'Now that's strange,' I said. 'I reckon he's been there for close on twenty-five years and he's only made lieutenant. I'd have thought a guy as good as you say would have been captain long before now.'

'Yeah, you're right. But there was something happened a while back and he got passed over twice. Reckon he'll stay just as he is now until they pension him off.'

'You know what it was that happened?'

'No — and I didn't ask. But it made

the papers. I was inside at the time and most of the guys in with me were pretty glad about it since he'd put most of 'em away.'

'Can you remember exactly when it was?' I waved the ten-dollar bill enticingly as bait.

He pushed his lips together. 'Reckon it must have been four, no five, years ago. Somebody pulled some strings with the Mayor at the time. Come to think of it, there was a rumor that Galecci had put a word into the Mayor's ear about Donovan. Elections were coming up around that time.'

'Thanks, Rusty.' I pushed the bill into his tight little fist. 'I guess I owe you one. Just keep all of this to yourself.'

'Sure thing.' He thrust the bill into his pocket and leaned further forward over the bar. 'I know when to keep my mouth shut.'

I hoped he did. If any word of my talking to him got out, he'd have not only Delano but Donovan on his back and whichever got to him first, it certainly wouldn't go easy on him.

That was the trouble with guys like Rusty. They made something on the side providing information to the cops or guys like me but sooner or later, the big boys they spilled the crap on got to hear about it and then the Rustys of this world disappeared, suddenly and quietly.

I crossed the street to where I'd parked the car, intending to drive to the newspaper office. I knew one of the editors there and figured he could soon find me the back copies, which might give me a little more information on why Donovan had been passed over for promotion. Where it fitted into this case, I wasn't sure. But those little mice still running around inside my brain were whispering that it might prove useful to know just what the reason was.

The street was almost deserted. A few prowlers were around on the sidewalks but this place didn't really come alive until after dark.

I'd almost reached the car when there was this sudden roar near the right intersection a couple of hundred yards away. Some instinct made me look round.

The car was doing at least fifty and the driver wasn't just joy-riding for the fun of it.

He had somebody in mind and it didn't take a genius to work out who it was. The Buick was coming straight at me. I just had a glimpse of the two men in the front and then reflex took over. Somehow, my legs moved themselves and I was diving forward. I hit the front wheel of the Merc, twisted, and flung myself in front of it, pressing myself so hard into the road I almost melted into it.

The Buick slammed against the side of the Merc and I felt the wind of its passing as I rolled over and pulled the .38 from its holster. I loosed off a couple of snap shots, hitting one of the rear tires with both slugs.

Somehow, I pushed myself to my feet as the car slewed sideways, careered over a fire hydrant and then ploughed into the front of a small delicatessen. Glass flew everywhere like confetti. One of the doors popped open and the passenger staggered out. He was a big guy and there was a gun in his hand.

He pointed it in my direction and a second later there was the thin whine of a slug ricocheting off the grille of the Merc an inch above my shoulder. Before I could bring up the .38, he had vanished around the corner. I walked slowly towards the wreck, my finger itching on the trigger.

The driver was slumped over the steering wheel. He was looking through the smashed windscreen but he wasn't seeing anything. Not with all that blood on his shirt and the wheel pushed deep into his chest. He wouldn't be seeing anything any more.

If Rusty was right, it hadn't taken long for Delano to act. A small crowd had gathered from nowhere, staring open-mouthed at the dead guy behind the wheel. A patrol car was on the scene within minutes.

One of the cops obviously recognized me. He walked over while his companion bent to examine the body through the car window, then walked around the wreck to peer closely at the rear wheel.

'You got any idea what happened here,

Merak?' the first cop asked. He was a tall guy, tough, with eyes like drills and a face that said he'd be pushed around by nobody.

'None at all,' I replied, keeping my voice as even as possible. 'The car just appeared from nowhere and tried to run me down. Then his pal took a shot at me before running off.'

'Seems to me you invite trouble no matter where you go.' He grinned but there was no humor in it.

The other cop came back. He jerked a thumb towards the Buick. 'A couple of slugs in the back tire,' he said laconically. 'It must have blown out straight away. If he was traveling at speed, he'd have had no chance of controlling it. Better get the morgue wagon for him.'

The cop standing directly in front of me nodded. But he didn't take his eyes away from my face. 'You got any idea why this guy should try to kill you?'

'Maybe he didn't like my face. Maybe someone else didn't like it and paid him to do it.'

'And maybe you're into something

right up to your neck.' The big man smiled again. 'These people don't put a hit on someone for nothing. You must have got up somebody's nose.'

'I guess I've done that with plenty of people,' I told him. I was beginning to feel uncomfortable. At the moment, I didn't fancy being hauled down to the precinct to answer a lot of fool questions. Even though they had nothing to pin on me, they could make things unpleasant if they had a mind to.

Finally, the big cop made up his mind. 'All right, Merak. You can go. But watch yourself from now on. We don't like trouble like this. Let me give you some good advice. Whatever trough you've got your nose into, take it out and stick to helping little old ladies find their runaway husbands. That way you might live a little longer.'

'I'll certainly bear that in mind, officer,' I said politely.

I walked back to the Merc. The Buick had scraped most of the paintwork when it had side-swiped it, but there didn't appear to be any real damage.

6

The newspaper offices were situated in a large white-stone building on the corner of the block at the intersection of Twenty-Fourth Street and James.

Fortunately, there was a spare space in front just waiting for me to drive into. A few people on the sidewalk paused to stare at the fresh scrapes along the side of the Merc, then hurried on as I glared at them.

Ed Carson's office was on the fourth floor. He was sitting behind his desk, his legs propped on top, chair tilted back and a half-smoked cigar between his lips. He'd just put down the phone when I pushed open the door and went in.

'Don't you ever knock, Johnny?' he grunted.

'Only when I'm not in a hurry,' I said.

He grinned. 'You're always in a goddamn hurry.' He gave me an appraising look. 'You'll forgive me for saying so, but you look as though you've been through the wars.'

'I guess you could say that, Ed. I've been on the wrong side of some guy who tried to run me down in the street. I've been shot at and warned off by a couple of cops who reckon I'm hustling in on their private territory. Apart from that it's been a nice day so far.'

'So what can I do for you to make it better?'

'I'd like to look through some of your back copies. There's something I'm not too happy about.'

Carson bent and opened the bottom drawer of his desk. He fished out a half full bottle of Scotch and a couple of glasses. He held the bottle up.

'Too early in the day for a drink?'

I shook my head. 'I guess it's never too early.'

He poured some into a glass and pushed it across to me. 'Now, how far back do you want to go?'

'Four, maybe five, years. I'm looking for something about Charles Donovan.'

He looked surprised at that. 'Lieutenant Charles Donovan — Homicide?'

'The same.' I lit a cigarette and sipped the whiskey appreciatively. It tasted good.

'Christ!' He rubbed his chin as if what I'd said was the most stupid and unnatural thing in the world. 'You're investigating him? What in hell's name for?'

'In a way, I suppose I am investigating him. From what I've heard he was one of the best detectives in Homicide but then something happened. Since then he's been passed over twice for captain and most of the time he acts as if the whole world's against him. Maybe there's nothing in this but it's one loose end I've got to tie up. Otherwise I won't sleep soundly at night.'

He digested that for a minute and then relit the cigar, which had gone out. He looked at it, then back at me. 'I won't ask anything about the case you're on, Johnny. That's your business. We've been friends for a long time. But I will say this. If you're serious about poking into Donovan's past life, you'd better watch your back.'

I finished my drink and set the glass on

the desk. 'I'll do that, Ed. Now, do you still have any copies going back to five years ago?'

'Sure. We should have them all. I'll get someone to dig them out for you.' He looked around the office. 'You can go through them over there.' He pointed to a small table near the side of the window. 'Nobody will bother you there.'

'Thanks.'

He went to the door and yelled somebody's name that I didn't catch. A young guy in his early twenties got up from behind one of the desks and came running over. Carson spoke to him for a couple of minutes and then came back.

'They'll be here in a little while,' he said. 'I suppose you know it'll take you hours to go through all of them to find what you want?'

I nodded. 'I'm not going anywhere in a hurry.'

When the first batch of newspapers arrived, I knew what Carson meant.

This was going to be like looking for the proverbial needle in a haystack. I settled myself comfortably in the chair at the table. I hadn't realized how much one year's editions of a newspaper stacked up to.

Still, I'd get nowhere just sitting looking at them. I picked up the first and scanned the headlines, ignoring the sports section and comic strips.

There was nothing there concerning Donovan. Still, I hadn't expected to hit the jackpot with the first shot.

Twenty minutes, half an hour, and I still hadn't come across a glimpse of his name. Maybe Rusty had been wrong, or maybe he didn't know anything and had just fed me that story to get his hands on that dough and get me out of his hair.

The young lad brought in a second batch and placed them neatly beside the others. Now I recognized just what I was up against. I rubbed my eyes and sat back for a moment. The print was beginning to dance in front of my eyes.

Carson had placed an ashtray on the side of the table and I lit a cigarette, wondering if I wasn't wasting my time.

'There's one more pile left for that year, sir.' The young employee was standing hesitantly behind me. 'Do you want me to bring them?'

I stared hard at those on the table, then shook my head. 'Leave them for the time being,' I told him. 'If I don't find what I'm looking for in these, I'll let you know.'

From his manner, I guessed he thought I had to be someone really important. But then, he'd probably only just started in the job and anyone who was on speaking terms with Carson was only just a little short of God Almighty.

As it turned out, I didn't have to call for the third batch to locate what I wanted. It was there on one of the inside pages of the edition dated June eighteenth.

It was headed:

HOMICIDE DETECTIVE DONOVAN SMASHES LA DOPE GANG.

I read it through twice so as not to miss anything. It made interesting reading although at the time, it might have been nothing out of the ordinary.

Apparently Donovan had spent more

than four months gathering evidence against a drug gang operating in downtown LA. Acting on information from an undercover cop, the police squad had trailed the gang to a large warehouse and had swooped just as the switch was being made to another fleet of trucks. The leader of the gang had been Sergio Galecci, Carlos' nephew.

When the cops had smashed their way into the warehouse, Sergio and a couple of others had tried to make a break for it but they hadn't got very far. There had been a car waiting at the rear of the warehouse and Sergio had picked up a couple of slugs in the back as he'd made a run for it. One of the bullets had shattered a vertebrae in his spine leaving him paralyzed from the waist down. He'd spent a couple of years in a secure prison hospital before someone, almost certainly his uncle, had pulled strings and he'd been deported back to Italy.

I sat back and stubbed out my cigarette. Things were beginning to make a little sense now. Bits of the jigsaw were slotting into place and the little mice in my head were having a field day. Even though it hadn't been Donovan who'd shot Sergio, he had been the man in charge of the operation that had led to him collecting that slug in the spine.

Carlos must have hated Donovan like poison after that. It was little wonder Donovan had never made captain. I reckoned that the decent, honest citizens of LA would have put him forward for a commendation. But they weren't the people who made the policies and pulled the strings. It was the men in the shadows, men like Carlos Galecci, who saw to it that only the politicians they backed got into power at election time.

Carlos would have thought twice about having Donovan kicked out of Homicide. That could have been political suicide for the Mayor and D.A. at the time. Donovan would have been a local hero with the townsfolk. But Galecci could see to it that he was never promoted, no matter how good he was in his job.

I figured it wouldn't have taken Donovan long to guess who was behind his stay as a mere lieutenant and from that moment on he would be a very bitter man.

'Find anything?' Ed spoke up from behind his desk.

'Plenty,' I told him. 'Although how relevant it is, I'm not sure.'

He walked over and glanced over my shoulder, rapidly scanning the page. 'So you figure it was Carlos who sat on Donovan's chances for any promotion?'

'Sure looks that way,' I agreed.

He straightened up with a grunt. 'Then why didn't he just quit the force at the time? Too old, maybe. Or it could be that Galecci would put the word around and it would follow him like a curse wherever he went.'

I had other ideas about that but I didn't come out with them. They needed a lot of thinking about.

There was a knock on the door and the young lad poked his head in. 'Do you want me to fetch that last batch of newspapers?' he asked.

I shook my head. 'Leave them,' I said. 'I reckon I've got what I need right here.'

I turned to Carson. 'Could you run off

a copy of this article for me, Ed?'

'Sure thing. You'll have it in a couple of minutes.'

He was as good as his word. I folded it carefully and put it into my inside pocket. At the moment, I'd no idea what to make of it. It certainly added another candidate to the list of those who'd had a grudge against Galecci. But without a lot more hard facts, that proved nothing.

'Anything else I can do for you, Johnny?' Ed asked.

'Nothing I can think of at the moment. You've been a great help.'

'Any time.' He showed me out.

When I let myself into the office, it was a little after three. Dawn jerked a thumb towards my desk.

'There was a phone call for you just over an hour ago. Manzelli wants to meet you tonight. They gave an address and you're to be there at eight-thirty prompt. Apparently it's something important and you're to go alone.'

I read the note she'd written. The words were exactly what she'd just said. 'Was it Manzelli himself who phoned?'

'I've no idea. Whoever it was, they didn't identify themselves. I couldn't detect any trace of a foreign accent.'

'Probably one of his stooges.' I read the message again. 'Or — '

'Or what?'

'I'm not sure.' I stared at the address she'd written down. It was somewhere way out in the suburbs. Not a residential address. 'This isn't like Manzelli. He hardly ever leaves that mansion of his. If he'd wanted to see me, I reckon he'd have me taken there.'

'You think it might not be him?' Dawn was beginning to sound worried.

'That's something I won't find out until I go.'

'And if it's not him, you could be walking into a trap. I'd think twice about this if I were you.'

'I am thinking about it,' I said. 'Either this message is genuine and Manzelli does have something on his mind, or it's something Delano has cooked up hoping to get rid of me before I can cause any more trouble.'

'Then you could be in deadly danger if

you're stupid enough to go.'

'Sure. And I'll be in just as much danger if it is from Manzelli and I don't turn up.'

'So what are you going to do?'

I shrugged. 'I don't have much choice, do I?'

She let it go at that.

* * *

I leaned back against the car seat and lit a cigarette, winding down the window. It was dark now and the nearest street lamp was almost out of sight more than two hundred yards away. I'd had little difficulty finding the place from what Dawn had written down. It was an empty warehouse on a small industrial site well away from any residential area and well off the main thoroughfares.

Tall steel pillars dotted the floor, stretching up to support the corrugated iron roof. The side spaces around them were all empty except for oil spills and the usual rubbish found in such places. Evidently the warehouse hadn't been in use for a long time.

I surveyed it minutely through the windscreen, flicking the ash from my cigarette out of the window. I had parked the Merc as close in one corner as possible where it wouldn't be readily spotted by anyone driving in. I'd switched off the engine and headlights, hoping that if it was a trap, I might get out of there before any shooting started up in earnest.

The more I thought about it, the more unlikely it seemed that Manzelli would choose a place like this for a meeting. There was something here that wasn't right but I couldn't put my finger on it. Maybe I was getting too suspicious in my old age. But there had already been two attempts on my life and I was superstitious enough not to want risking a third.

Flicking the cigarette butt out of the window, I watched it wink out, then checked my watch. It wanted ten minutes to eight-thirty. Getting out of the car, I closed the door quietly and eased my way along the wall to one of the pillars.

I checked the .38 and eased it gently in its holster. The silence was beginning to get oppressive as if a storm was gathering outside, ready to break at any moment. I checked my watch again. Three minutes to go if whoever had made that phone call was on time.

The knot in the middle of my stomach tightened. There was no sound. The city traffic was far enough away to be non-existent. Even the rats were quiet as if holding their breath, waiting for something to happen.

Then a faint swathe of light showed across the wide opening to one side.

It grew brighter and I was able to make out the soft purr of a car engine. It was the low purring sound made by one of the top-of-the-range limousines, scarcely making any impact on the silence.

I threw a swift glance around the side of the pillar as the light grew brighter and then separated into twin beams as the limousine swung round and drove into the building. It stopped some forty yards away. The headlights died, as did the sound of the engine. No one got out. It just sat there, waiting. I could vaguely make out a solitary figure seated behind the wheel, enough to tell there was only one person in the car. Whoever it was, they had come alone and that wasn't like Manzelli.

That threw me a little. I thought, he'd never show up in a place like this without a couple of gunmen with him, even to meet me.

When no one showed, I stepped out from behind the pillar and walked slowly towards the car, keeping my right hand around the .38. I approached the car from the rear, taking care not to line myself up with either of the wing mirrors.

I was some ten feet away when the door opened and the driver got out.

There was the unmistakable click of high-heeled shoes on the concrete floor.

'Hello, Johnny. I'm so glad you decided to come. I figured that phone call might make you curious.'

Gloria Galecci!

Maybe I should have guessed it would be her. The way Dawn had handled her on that boat must have really rankled.

She stepped away from the car where I could see her clearly. She was wearing the same blue dress and there was a smile on her lips as she walked towards me. It was a smile that boded me no good. As far as I could make out she wasn't carrying a gun and that made me wonder if there were other hoodlums around in the shadows, waiting to jump out of the walls at the first wrong move I made.

'You know, Johnny. I thought we could have been good friends, maybe even lovers. Or wasn't the offer I made you good enough?'

'Oh, that sounded really good at the time,' I replied. 'But aren't you forgetting something? It was you who put me off the case when we met at your husband's funeral. I'd have been quite willing to carry on working for you. But after what happened on that yacht, I wouldn't trust you as far as I could throw you.'

She threw her head back at that and laughed. She came right up to me so that I could smell her perfume. 'The offer still stands. Just give up this case, forget all about how and why Carlos died and go back to your mundane, everyday little cases and I'll make it well worth your while.'

'Not a chance,' I said. 'I'm sticking with this case right to the end. I guess I owe Carlos that much. And if you obviously know about Manzelli, I reckon you know I've got some influential friends at my back.'

She shook her head. 'Too bad. I see I've seriously misjudged you. An honest private detective who can't be bribed. It makes you think there's some good in this world, after all.' Her eyes glinted in the dimness like chips of ice.

Without warning, her right arm came up and a bunched fist caught me on the side of the face, knocking me sideways against the boot of the limousine.

Somehow, I kept my feet and pulled out the .38 but before I could get it clear of my overcoat, her stiffened hand slammed hard on my wrist. My arm went numb and the gun went flying across the concrete.

I tried to yell but no sound came out. I'd never hit a woman before but I'd seen what she was capable of and this was no time for knightly chivalry.

My left fist connected with her chin. It was a good solid punch with most of my weight behind it. Her head went back but she didn't go down. Before I could land another she had straightened up, her lips drawn back from her teeth.

I started to back away but she was too fast. Her hands lashed out, grabbing my legs and shoulders as she bent forward. The next second she had hoisted me across her shoulders. Her legs straightened and she was spinning me around. The walls of the warehouse, vague shadows in the gloom, whirled before my eyes in a dizzying circle. Then, with an upward heave of her arms, she lifted me over her head, held me there for a few seconds, and threw me onto the bonnet of the car. I hit it with a jar that knocked all of the breath out of me.

But I'd been thrown like that before. I hit the bonnet sideways and rolled with the impact, somehow landing on my feet on the other side. I pulled myself up. Already, she was coming around the front of the limousine. The look on her face told me she didn't mean to stop until she'd killed me. It was going to be either her or me.

Getting my legs under me, I swung myself back onto the bonnet, balancing myself on the smooth surface. For a moment, she stopped, not sure what I intended doing next.

I'd seen plenty of the wrestling shows on television, had watched some of the moves those guys made. Now, I flung myself down at her, twisting my body sideways so that I hit her across the chest. I expected her to go down under the impact but she was too damned strong. The breath went out of her mouth in a loud gasp as she caught me with her arms. But she was still on her feet.

Somehow, I got my arm against her throat and pushed hard. The only effect it had was to make her take a step backward. But it proved to be enough. She uttered a stifled yell as her foot slipped on a patch of oil. Unable to help herself, she fell back and I heard her head crack loudly on the concrete floor. Her arms fell away. For a full minute, I lay there with her pinned under me, pulling air into my lungs before thrusting myself to my feet.

Her eyes were closed and I figured that crack on the skull might have killed her. Bending, I felt for the pulse. It was still beating strongly and she was still breathing raggedly. She'd live, but I knew she'd never forget. Gloria Galecci had but one mission in life and that was to finish me — permanently.

I left her lying there. This was the time to leave, to go far away and as quickly as possible. I walked over to where my gun lay on the floor, slipped it into its holster, and threw one more glance at Gloria, lying there beside her car. I knew she'd be out cold for a while. She was possibly dreaming she was still coming after me, but this time with a gun in her hand.

I started towards my car, then stopped. I couldn't be sure whether Gloria had planned this on her own, or whether she had persuaded Delano to let her finish me herself. One thing was certain. It hadn't been her who had made that phone call. So there was someone else in this with her, someone who knew just what she had in mind.

I thought it over and then walked to the wide opening. An inch at a time, I levered my head around the steel upright. The long roadway between the buildings was almost empty. Nothing moved but at the far end, near the junction with another of the road that criss-crossed the site, a dark, slim shape stood. No lights showed but I recognized it as a car similar to Gloria's, big and powerful. It was capable of covering that distance in less than ten seconds with the engine fully revved up.

Checking that Gloria was still out, I went quickly to the opposite opening. They had another car parked there at the far end, sitting ready to move at a moment's notice.

But there was one thing they hadn't taken into account. Straight in front of me was a narrow opening between two tall buildings. It was barely more than a passage but from what I could see it stretched away into the distance, probably intersecting half a dozen or more of the roads running lengthwise across the site.

Maybe I could make it, maybe not. But it was the only chance I had.

I ran back to the car and slipped behind the wheel, starting the engine.

Sooner or later, those guys would come looking for Gloria and I wanted to be out of there before that happened.

I eased the Merc slowly between the pillars not daring to switch on the headlights. I reached the entrance and paused with my foot off the accelerator. Then I jammed it down hard, aiming for the narrow gap almost directly opposite. I heard the wings scrape the buildings on both sides. Then I was gripping the wheel tightly and praying there were no out-jutting girders in the way.

I went across the next road, still driving straight ahead, when headlights showed briefly some distance behind me. Those guys waiting for me had been quick off the mark, too quick. They had completely missed the opening. Now they either had to reverse and try to follow me, or hope to cut me off somewhere on the perimeter of the site.

More metal shrieked like a banshee's

wail as the Merc scraped along the walls. I took a risk and switched on the headlights. They showed me that the route ahead was clear for at least a couple of hundred yards.

I crossed two more roads at right angles and then slammed on the brakes as I approached the third, swinging the car around in a tight semi-circle before hitting the road. It too was clear and I pushed the accelerator right to the floor.

Less than five minutes later, I was clear of the buildings, driving fast around the city limits. A minute later I picked up headlights behind me, closing fast. I kept my eye on them in the mirror. Fortunately there was no traffic around but I didn't want to attract the attention of any speed cop waiting out of sight in some side alley.

It was more than likely the guys following me would have a good story ready and the cops didn't like me anyway. They'd probably hand me over to them and forget to file a report about the matter.

At the corner of Eighteenth, I swung

sharp right. I had an idea that might pay off if the gods smiled on me. If not, it would be a bad end to a bad day. The road I was on led out of town, away into the hills. Behind me, the headlights stuck like glue. They weren't going to give up now.

Soon there were no buildings on either side of the road. Ahead of me the road started to climb. It was a gentle ascent at first, but I knew it would soon get steeper and there were some dangerously sharp bends a few miles further on. You had to know what you were doing driving along this road at speed after dark.

I was hoping the guys tailing me weren't just as familiar with this road as I was.

Ten minutes later, I hit the bottom of the hill and shifted the Merc into third gear. At my back, the headlights crept closer. I could imagine those guys trying to figure out what my game was, leading them away from town. They must have figured they could overtake me any time they wished. And they'd have only one thing in mind. To drive me off the road so that it would look like a tragic accident. Things like that happened all the time on this road.

I flicked my gaze back and forth from the rear mirror while trying to concentrate on my driving. Long wisps of fog started to chase me now. The road was still climbing, twisting and turning sharply without any warning apart from the white-painted fences strung along the edge of the drop.

For five minutes, the two cars kept an almost constant distance behind me. Their headlights wove back and forth as they followed the crazy contours of the road, splaying the rockface on one side with diffuse patches of light, disappearing into the darkness on the other. Then the leading car suddenly accelerated. I reckoned the men in it were beginning to get impatient. Maybe they figured we were far enough away from town for there to be no other traffic at this time of night.

I pressed a little harder on the accelerator. The engine roared. A moment later there was a sharp crack behind me. I heard the wicked hum of the slug past my ear and ducked down behind the wheel. I knew I had to act fast now. If they managed to hit one of the tires, I'd be waking up with the angels.

Up ahead, a hundred yards away, the road swung left through almost ninety degrees. Swathes of fog now drifted lazily in front of me, throwing the light from the headlights back at me.

I slowed deliberately. Within seconds, the car at my back rammed me hard from behind. The jerk almost pushed me out of the seat. He dropped back a little, ready to accelerate again. It was the moment I was waiting for.

Praying that the driver had been paying too much attention to slamming me from the rear, and not enough attention on the road, I swung the wheel sharply, pressing my foot down on the accelerator pedal as far as it would go.

As I'd hoped, the move took him completely by surprise. I felt the tires skid on the rough surface. The right wing touched the wooden fence. Then I managed to straighten up and guide the Merc into the middle of the road.

Through the mirror I saw the limousine plough straight into the fence. It smashed it like a row of matchsticks. Then it was in the air as if it had been kicked from behind. The nose went down as it soared out of control over the edge.

The second car was already too close for the driver to brake in time. I saw it slew sideways and somehow come to a halt. The nearside wheels were over the rim of the drop-off. It was tilted crazily like a crab on one leg, hanging onto the edge of the hill. From somewhere out of sight, an expanding orange flare illuminated the fog.

Gently, I eased the Merc to the top of the hill and pulled into one side. Down below, the wreck of the first car was burning furiously at the bottom of the hill where it had somersaulted and smashed onto the rocks. I could just make out a couple of figures hovering around the second. But they wouldn't be going anywhere unless they walked.

I reckoned I'd have no more trouble from them. I wasn't sure whose men they were, but whoever it was, he was going to be pretty sore at how they had botched everything. I didn't know how many men had been in the first car; all I knew was they wouldn't be walking out of it.

I checked the Merc for damage as best I could in the foggy darkness. More of the paintwork was gone and there was a neat bullet hole in the rear window. Still, it could have been worse. I reckoned I'd got off pretty lightly considering all that had happened.

Getting back into the car, I took a wide detour out of the hills and drove back to town. There was no point in going back to the office. I'd report what had happened in the morning. Not that anyone would do anything about it. Just one of those things associated with the job.

I drove to Dawn's instead. I needed a drink and a good night's sleep before I was ready to face the world again.

7

There was nothing in any of the papers the next morning concerning an accident on the hill road outside of town. I hadn't expected anything. Either it hadn't been reported or if the cops knew anything about it they'd been told to ignore it. Either way, it had been hushed up.

Dawn had made breakfast for me and we'd driven together to my office. She'd cast a critical eye over the Merc when we'd left her place but had said nothing. I'd told her some of what had happened, but not about Gloria Galecci. That episode was something I wasn't too proud about, maybe something to do with the male ego.

Once in the office, I went through the papers again but the result was just the same as before. For all the world knew, the events of the previous night had never happened.

'It doesn't make any sense,' Dawn said.

'What is it they think you know about Galecci's death?'

'Obviously it's something important and I've got a feeling it's something to do with our visit to Tefler. He knew something as well, something he got killed for. And now they're out to get me.'

'You really think that?'

She stared hard at me. I pushed the newspapers to one side of the desk.

'Of course I think it,' I said. 'I didn't have a chance to check out that vault when we found Galecci's body. So it's not that. Somehow, Tefler is the key to all this.'

'You don't think he could have been the killer? Maybe one of Galecci's friends found out and killed him for revenge.'

'I have a feeling it's a little more complicated than that.'

'Why?' she asked. 'Aren't there any simple, uncomplicated cases?'

I shook my head. 'Not that you'd notice. And Tefler had no motive for killing Galecci. In fact, just the opposite. He must have made a lucrative business selling him all those antique clocks. You don't find many collectors like Galecci and when you do you want to hold on to them, not bump them off.'

'All right. So it wasn't him but — '

'But he was either in on it, or he knew who the killer was,' I interrupted. 'And somehow I think he knew he wouldn't live long with that knowledge inside his head.'

'So?'

'So we have to look at what kind of guy Tefler was. He wasn't a cold-blooded killer like Galecci, Rizzio or Delano. He was just an ordinary guy who got caught up in something nasty. How do you think a man like that would feel if he knew that his actions had resulted in someone being murdered?'

'Not very pleased with himself.'

'Exactly. And there was something I remember noticing at Galecci's funeral. Tefler crossed himself at the end of the service. He was a Catholic.'

Dawn looked puzzled. 'So what difference does that make?'

'It could make one hell of a difference. If he keeps that knowledge to himself and allows a killer to go unpunished, it's a mortal sin. What's the first thing a Catholic would do with something like that on his conscience? He'd go to confession and tell it all to the priest.'

'But that would mean — '

'That it would all come out? There's no chance that would happen. The priest could never disclose whatever was said during confession. Even the law can't force him to do that and Tefler would know it.'

'I still don't see what you're getting at, Johnny.'

'Just this.' I settled myself back in my chair. 'Tefler might confess everything in the confessional knowing it could never be disclosed. But it's my guess the priest would tell him to go to the police and tell them everything before he'd give him absolution. But as far as we know, he didn't do that.'

'And you think you know why?'

'I'm trying hard to figure that out and the only answer I can come up with is that he daren't. Either he knew, or maybe just suspected, that Donovan was in on the plot too. And it's my bet he couldn't keep it to himself for long. His conscience wouldn't let him. He had to confide in someone, someone he trusted completely.'

'And I suppose you've even figured out who that might be?' Her voice was warm and sarcastic at the same time.

'If I'm right, there's only one person. His good friend for twenty-five years, Simon Bergstein, the tailor next door.'

Dawn's eyes grew wide. 'Then my God, if you're right, Bergstein is in danger too. It won't take long for the real killer to work this out too. Even if you're wrong, the murderer can't take any chances of him talking to someone.'

'And if I'm right, Bergstein is the only lead we've got.'

'You think you can get to him and make him talk before the killer does?'

I got up and jammed my hat on my head. 'Unless we want another killing on our hands, I've got to.'

Dawn thought for a minute, then said, 'You going to drive across town in your car? Somebody wants you dead as much as Bergstein and in the state your car is, you might just as well advertise yourself from the top of City Hall.'

She was right. I'd been a sitting target once in the last twenty-four hours. There seemed no point in repeating the performance. I phoned for a cab and waited inside the doorway downstairs until it slid to a halt in front of the building.

'Main Street,' I said to the driver.

He accelerated away without a word. Normally, whenever I took a cab I got one of those talkative guys who give you all the latest news on football, world affairs, what's wrong with America and LA in particular, and who's sleeping with who's wife among the top echelon of politicians. This guy made a refreshing change and I settled back to enjoy the silence.

We hit a little traffic on the way but twenty minutes later I was deposited outside Bergstein's shop. I gave the driver a five dollar bill and told him to keep the change. He lowered his head and peered through the window and spoke for the first time.

'You sure this is the place you're looking for, bud? It looks all closed up to me.'

I turned and looked at the shop for the first time. He was right. There was a card hanging in the middle of the window. It said: CLOSED UNTIL FURTHER NOTICE.

'You want me to wait?'

I shook my head. 'I'll take a look around,' I said.

'Suit yourself.' He drove off leaving me standing there, wondering what the hell to do next. Maybe I should have seen it coming. Bergstein had been a frightened man when I'd last spoken to him. If Tefler had told him everything it would have left him thinking and when Tefler had been murdered that would have been the last straw for him.

I knocked loudly on the door twice. I didn't expect anything to happen and nothing did. The shop was as empty as Lazarus' tomb. Beside it, the cops had removed the tape from around Tefler's place. Evidently they'd finished their search of the premises and gone.

I was hammering vainly on the door a second time when a voice called from the opposite side of the street. I turned. A woman was standing in the doorway of the house directly across from Bergstein's. She beckoned and I walked over.

'You looking for Mister Bergstein's?' she asked. She had that look about her. The kind of person who knows everything and misses nothing. If you want to know anything, they're the ones to approach. The only difficulty is separating fact from fantasy and exaggeration.

I gave a brief nod. 'It's urgent that I speak to him,' I said. 'It's very important. Do you have any idea where he is?'

'He left yesterday. Around noon, it was. I must say he seemed to be in a hurry.'

'But do you have any idea where he went?'

'He never said.' She eyed me up and down, missing nothing about me. I figured she had me down as someone looking for money from him.

I took out my card and handed it to her. She turned it over once or twice, then peered short-sightedly at it. 'You a detective? Now why didn't you say so in the first place? What's he wanted for?'

'It's nothing he's done,' I told her. 'I just want to ask him a few questions, that's all.'

She looked a little disappointed at that and changed the subject. 'Is it about the murder? Poor Mister Tefler. He was a real gentleman. Always had a good word for everybody.'

'Did you see anything that night?'

Her mouth puckered. 'I was out.' The disappointment showed through in her voice. 'By the time I got back, it was all over. I did see the police car outside the shop and two people come out.'

'Did you see who they were?'

'A man and a woman. I'd say the man was about your size but I couldn't describe either of them accurately. My eye sight ain't too good without my glasses.'

I knew she was describing Dawn and myself. Clearly it was useless asking her about anything that had happened prior to that. I returned to my original line of questioning.

'Mister Bergstein. Do you know of any relatives he may have gone to stay with?'

'Relatives?' Her mouth tightened as she thought about that. Then she gave an almost imperceptible nod. 'He did talk once or twice about a brother — lives somewhere on the other side of town. But from what he said, they weren't all that close. I don't think there was anyone else.'

'You wouldn't happen to know where, exactly, on the other side of town?'

'I've no idea. He didn't speak of him often.'

'Okay,' I pointed to my card, which she still held in her hand. 'If you do think of anything else, just call that number. You can leave a message with my secretary if I'm not there.'

Her eyes lit up a little at that. If she could have puffed out her chest any further, she would have done.

I turned back to the sidewalk. My talk with this witness seemed to have reached a dead end. Then she called loudly, 'There is one other thing. I've just remembered Mister Bergstein telling me that his brother's name is Manny. Reckon that's short for Emmanuel, ain't it?'

'I reckon it is,' I replied.

It helped but not as much as I'd have liked. My only chance of finding this Emmanuel Bergstein was through the city telephone directory and there was the possibility that quite a number of people with that name would be listed.

It was a long shot, any longer and I'd have said there was no chance at all.

I went back to the office. Dawn gave me an inquiring look as I went in and threw my hat onto the desk. When I said nothing, she broke the silence.

'Well? Did you see him?'

'No. He's closed up shop and skipped out.'

'So what can you do now?'

'Fortunately there was the local busy-body just across the street. She seemed anxious to talk once she learned I was a private dick. Seems Bergstein left in a hurry yesterday. He had only one relative, a brother he doesn't get on with too well. But my guess is he's prepared to let bygones be bygones just so long as he gets help to vanish off the face of the earth.'

'You think he's that scared?'

'I'm sure he is. Now all I have to do is locate this brother who lives somewhere on the other side of LA.'

'How?'

'Through the city directory. His first name's Emmanuel. If there are more than one listed, it'll have to be a process of elimination.'

As luck would have it, there was only one Emmanuel Bergstein listed. He lived at 1266 East 24th Place. I jotted the address down on my cigarette pack.

This looked too easy to be true. I reached for my hat.

'Wouldn't it be quicker to ring him?' Dawn asked. 'Even though he's the only one listed, he might not be the man you're looking for.'

'That would be a rather stupid thing to do. If he is Bergstein's brother and I ring, asking questions, he's going to deny knowing him and the second I get off the phone he'll warn his brother and you won't see Bergstein's heels for the dust.

He'll just fade into the sunset and I'll never find him.'

'I guess you're right.'

'I am. Now get me a cab. I can't risk taking the Merc on this job.'

Dawn sighed. 'I wouldn't like to see your expenses at the end of the month,' she said as she reached for the phone.

The cab was waiting for me as I reached the sidewalk. Getting into the back, I gave the address to the driver and settled back in the seat. As we drove through the city center I kept a close watch on our rear. There was no sign of another vehicle acting strangely, weaving in and out of the traffic, so I felt fairly confident I wasn't being followed.

★ ★ ★

The address was a small house, indistinguishable from all of the others in the street. It looked as though it had seen better days, like a tired old lady sitting in a rocking chair, waiting to die.

I got out and told the driver to wait. He looked dubious but he didn't argue. The bell worked, but only just. I could scarcely hear it through the door. There was no answer but the curtain twitched slightly in the window at the side. I rang again, keeping my finger on the button.

After a couple of minutes, there came the faint sound of footsteps and the door opened a couple of inches.

I said, 'Mister Bergstein? Mister Emmanuel Bergstein?'

'Yes. What do you want?'

'The name's Merak. I'm a private detective. May I come in and talk? It's vitally important.'

I saw him hesitate. He stared hard at me for a long, uncomfortable minute. Then with an effort, he opened the door wider and motioned me inside.

I stepped through the door while he turned and closed it behind me. The radio in one corner of the front room was on. One of the music programs. He walked over and switched it off. From the appearance of the room I guessed that he was either widowed or a bachelor. There was no evidence of a woman's touch anywhere. Everything was basic and purely functional.

'I don't understand what this is about, Mister Merak,' he said. He waved a negligent hand towards a faded chintz chair. A bogus smile twitched like a shadow across his lips. It was gone within seconds.

I sat down and leaned back against the hardness of the chair. It was obvious he was scared and trying hard not to show it. Simon Bergstein had looked old but this man was even older. He could have given Methusalah a few years.

'I'm here about your brother, Simon,' I said, watching his face closely for any reaction. 'I spoke to him only a couple of days ago. But his shop is closed now and there's no sign of him.'

He made no attempt to deny that Simon Bergstein was his brother. His eyes were not as vague as when he had opened the door to me. There was now a sharpness in them as if he was weighing me up and wondering how much I knew.

'Simon's not here if that's what you want to know. I haven't spoken to him for more than three years. Just what is it he's done for you to have taken this interest in him?'

'I'm afraid your brother is in very grave danger. Not from me,' I hastened to assure him. 'But there are men after him who'll stop at nothing to silence him. Unless I can get to him first, I'm afraid he'll end up on a slab in the mortuary.'

I studied his face intently. Strangely, that news didn't seem to surprise him as it should have. I knew then that Simon had been in touch with him and had told him something of what had happened.

'Are you in with the police?' he asked finally.

I shook my head. 'The cops and I don't get on very well together,' I told him. 'They figure I'm pushing in on their territory. Believe me, I've no intention of turning him over to them. All I want to do is ask him a few questions.'

I took out a cigarette, lit it, and waited. Either he knew where his brother was, or he didn't. If he did he would either tell me or he wouldn't. It was as simple as that.

'All right,' he said finally. 'Simon did

ring me yesterday. Said something about his friend next door who'd been murdered. He thought the police had the idea he knew something about it but he didn't trust them, said they were just as bad as the mobs who'd probably carried out the killing.'

'That makes sense,' I said. 'You can't trust anybody these days. Everyone's in it for the take.' I'd already made up my mind that wherever Simon was, he wasn't holed up in this house. I'd found his brother easily enough and it wouldn't take the killer much longer to do the same.

'Do you know where your brother is?' I asked.

'No. And I don't want to know.' He tried to put a lot of indignation into his tone, too much to be genuine.

'You're absolutely sure about that?'

'Of course, I'm sure. If he's got any sense he'll be out of this town and heading west, or east, or anywhere.'

'He's a fool if he tries that,' I said. 'There's nowhere far enough for him to run when these boys are after you.'

'That's his lookout. I don't know what trouble he's got himself into, but I want nothing to do with it.'

He was lying, of course. I'd seen too many of his type not to have spotted it right away. He knew exactly where his brother was holed up. But there was no way he was going to tell me.

I got up. 'Well, thank you for your time, Mister Bergstein. If you should hear from your brother, tell him it's vital he should get in touch with me right away.' I gave him my card.

He looked at it for a moment, then put it down on the table.

He followed me to the door and stood there. The cab driver was reading a newspaper. He pushed it down between the front seats as I got in.

Leaning forward, I said, 'Drive around the corner yonder and stop just out of sight.'

He nodded as if he got this request every day. Quite a guy, I thought. I was lucky to have got him. A man who did as he was asked without asking funny questions.

Once around the corner, I got out and walked back to the intersection. I could see along the whole length of the street without being spotted by Bergstein. There was a chance he'd just ring his brother and tell him about me asking awkward questions. But I was banking on him doing something else.

That was exactly what he did.

Less than five minutes later a cab came along the street and stopped outside his house. He came out almost at once. Evidently he had been waiting for it just inside the doorway. He got into it and closed the door quickly.

I sprinted back to my own cab, jumped in and told the driver to head back and follow the other. He did it without a word. The way he kept a good distance and yet remained close enough not to lose the other cab told me this wasn't the first time he'd done something like this.

I reckoned he was an old hand at this game. Even if Bergstein had been watching, I doubted if he'd known we were tailing him. Very soon we were past the suburbs and heading for open country. Now things became a little more tricky. The driver dropped back, easing his foot off the pedal.

'Do you know anything of this area?' I asked.

He gave a nod. 'I know it as well as the back of my hand. Used to come here as a kid.'

Up ahead, perhaps half a mile away, the cab in front suddenly swung left and disappeared behind thick hedges.

'Where does that road go to?' I pointed.

'It ain't a road, mister. Just a track. Goes up the hill for maybe a quarter of a mile. There are some cabins there. Folk sometimes come here during the summer for the fishing. Reckon most of 'em will be empty now.'

We crawled to where the track branched off. I told the driver to let me off and then go along the road for a way and park out of sight.

I checked the gun butt under my arm and walked forward. The track was so narrow I wondered how that other cab had made it. The ditches on either side had a few inches of dirty brown water in them. The faint gurgle of the water running downhill was the only sound.

I went up around a curve and then into the trees. A couple of minutes later, I spotted the cab parked sideways in front of one of the cabins. The driver was sitting behind the wheel looking at nothing. There was no sign of Emmanuel Bergstein.

The cabin door was closed but I caught a movement behind the single window and guessed my hunch had paid off. A quick look round told me there were no telephone lines for miles so Emmanuel wouldn't have been able to phone his brother even if the thought had occurred to him. This place was as primitive as any in the state.

Ducking down, I skirted around the cabin, checking there was no other exit. I figured neither of the brothers would be capable of fleeing out of the window.

A stoop ran along the front of the cabin and there was an old rocker near the door. I eased the .38 from its holster and held it ready. There were voices inside the cabin but I couldn't make out the words.

The cab driver had lit a cigarette and was sitting with the window down and his elbow resting on the door. Occasionally, he flicked ash outside. His back was to me and he seemed to be taking no interest in what was going on.

I walked up to the cabin door making no noise and paused for a moment with my hand around the handle. Then I pushed it open and stepped inside.

Simon Bergstein was seated on a faded settee in the middle of the room, his hands clasped around his knees. Emmanuel was over by the fireplace, his back to the wall.

They both jumped a foot into the air. I closed the door quietly.

'Now suppose we just have a quiet little talk,' I said. I held out the gun where they could see it but not pointed at them. They weren't going to give me any trouble.

'That was a stupid thing you did.' I looked directly at the man on the couch as I spoke. 'Running away like that. Now you have put yourself in real danger.'

'Just what is it you want?' Simon asked.

He unclasped his hands and made to get up. His face twisted as if his back hurt him.

'I'm here to try to save your life,' I told him. 'Maybe you don't believe that but it happens to be true.'

'How did you find us?' This time it was Emmanuel who spoke. He held himself very still against the wall as if he'd been painted on.

'That was no problem. I figured you'd help your brother once he'd explained the fix he's in. You did exactly as I expected you would. It wasn't difficult to tail you here. And if I could do it, you can be damned sure those other guys can. For all I know, they might be coming up that track this very minute.' I paused, then added grimly, 'And they'll be packing a lot more artillery than I am.'

Emmanuel made to go to the window, then thought better of it. He let his hands fall helplessly to his sides. I felt sorry for the two of them.

Unwittingly, they had become caught up in a dangerous situation not of their own making.

'How do we know we can trust you?' Simon asked.

I didn't say anything for a moment. Then I said, 'Right now, you have to trust someone. I figure you daren't go to the cops. And if what you know can put the finger on the guy who killed Carlos Galecci, I'm the only one you can trust.'

'That's easy to say.' Emmanuel snapped angrily.

'True,' I acknowledged. 'But think about it. I've got this gun. If I was the one after your brother, you'd both be dead now — and that goes for the cab driver outside. Nobody would find you until summer.'

I could see they were both thinking about that. Maybe it got through, maybe it didn't. But I didn't have enough time for them to debate about it.

'Don't take all day thinking about it,' I said harshly. 'Either wait here until those hitmen arrive — and believe me, they will — or come with me. I'll put a phone call through to a friend of mine and he does have the muscle to keep you safe until there's a trial.'

'You mean we'll have to give evidence in court?' Simon almost whispered.

'You certainly will.' I looked across at him. 'Because I'm damned sure that Tefler told you who killed Galecci.'

From the look on his face I knew I'd hit the nail on the head. And I knew he'd already decided to do exactly as I said. All I had to do was keep him alive until the killer could be brought to trial.

8

I put the gun away and went over to the window. Outside, everything seemed quiet, too quiet. The cab they had come in was still there, the driver staring out at nothing. I reckoned he could have sat there all day just so long as the meter was running.

'This might not be easy,' I said without turning my head. 'I don't think I was followed here but there's a chance those guys are smart. There could be a carload of them coming up that track this very minute.'

I crossed to the door and opened it a little way. For five minutes I listened to the wind rustling in the trees. A few crickets were chirping in the grass. But that was all. Then, some distance away, there was another sound. An automobile engine, and it could only be on that road somewhere down below.

I could see nothing for the trees and it

could have been just another car passing along the road at the bottom end of the track. I tried to follow the sound. It came from the direction of town and then the noise dropped suddenly in pitch and volume. That could mean only one thing. The driver had slowed sharply, changing down a gear, and from the direction I judged it was right where the track branched off the road.

'This could be trouble,' I said sharply. 'Now both of you do exactly as I say if you want to go on living.'

I motioned them to the door, out onto the stoop. Out of the corner of my eye I saw the driver make a movement. I reckon it was the first he'd made since he'd stopped there. He twisted his head sharply.

Simon started for the cab but I hauled him back. 'Not that way. That's just what they'll expect you to do. Get back into the trees and stay out of sight.'

They both stared at me. They were scared stiff and I thought they were going to burst into tears.

'Do as I say,' I hissed.

I spun Simon round and herded him forward. For a minute, I thought he was going to sit down and blubber like a kid but somehow he pulled himself together. Running awkwardly, he ran around the side of the cabin and vanished.

I ran over to the cab. The driver had opened his door and had one foot outside. He looked almost as scared as the brothers.

'What the hell — ?' he began.

'I'm a private detective,' I said harshly. 'Never mind about how I got here. Those two men are in deadly danger. I'm hoping to save their lives but you've got to do as I say. Got that?'

'Look mister, I don't know what's happening here, but — '

'There's no time for explanations. There's a car coming up that track right now and the men in it are out to kill those two before they can testify in a murder case before a grand jury. All I want you to do is wait until that car gets here. Then you put your foot on the accelerator and hightail it back down the track and into town. You don't stop for anything. Get that?'

'Sure, but I — '

'Just do as I say and you won't get hurt. Those guys won't want any witnesses around once they get here.'

That did it for him. He swung his leg back inside, shut the door, and turned the key in the ignition. I waited for a couple of seconds, then turned and ran for the trees. Simon and Emmanuel Bergstein were there, slumped against the trunk of one of the trees. They looked like Tweedledum and Tweedledee who had fallen off one of the branches.

'What now?' Emmanuel asked. His voice shook.

'Now we wait,' I said. 'If this pays off we may still get out of here. If not, someone may get hurt.' I took out the .38 and checked it. 'Now stay right here and don't make any noise.'

I slipped away through the trees to where I could just make out the open space in front of the cabin. Fifteen seconds later, a car appeared at the top of the track and made a sharp turn towards the cabin.

In the same moment, the cab driver revved up the engine and let in the clutch. He drove forward lifting dust from beneath the wheels as he spun the cab around the bend. His nearside wing scraped hard against the side of the other car. Then he was past and heading away as if Hell had suddenly opened up and all the devils were on his tail.

I was banking on whoever was in the car figuring Simon Bergstein was in the cab and making a getaway. It didn't take long to prove me right. A hand came through the car window. There was a gun in it and a couple of slugs followed the cab along the track. Moments later, the car executed a sharp turn, sliding in the dust. Then it was gone, racing down the hill.

I went back to the brothers. 'They fell for it,' I told them. 'We'll give them a couple of minutes to get well away from here. Then we leave.'

'And if they're waiting for us on the road?' Emmanuel queried.

I shrugged. 'Somehow, I reckon they'll follow that cab all the way into town. By the time they find out they've been duped, I hope to have your brother somewhere safe.'

We waited. There was no sound anywhere that had no right to be there.

Even the crickets seemed to have fallen silent. When I was satisfied the would-be assassins were far enough away, I said, 'Okay. Let's go.'

They both looked at me as if I was out of my mind. 'Do you expect us to walk all the way back into town?' Simon asked.

'That won't be necessary. We just walk down to the road. It isn't far.'

Neither of them spoke. Either they thought I was mad, or that maybe I had my own car stashed away somewhere out of sight.

We set off along the track. There were deep tire marks on one side where either the cab, or that car, had slid dangerously close to the ditch. Once we came within sight of the road, I stopped and motioned my two companions to do likewise. As far as I could see in both directions, it was empty. It looked as though my ruse had paid off.

We reached the bottom of the track and I walked out into the middle of the road. I couldn't see any sign of my cab but a few seconds later there was the unmistakable cough of an engine starting up and it appeared from somewhere among the trees a couple of hundred yards further on.

I put the brothers into the back and then seated myself next to the driver. I gave him Dawn's address. I knew it might be putting her into danger but it was the only place I could think of.

We arrived there half an hour later. She was still at the office and I used my own key after paying off the driver. Then I phoned her to let her know what had happened.

'Don't you think you should let Donovan know?' she asked. Her voice sounded calm but concerned. 'He phoned here an hour ago asking for you. Wanted to get in touch with you right away.'

'I bet he did. Bergstein doesn't want the cops brought in and I'm inclined to agree with him. Donovan is mixed up in this somewhere. Maybe he's covering up for the killer, I don't know.'

'Then what are you going to do? Sooner or later, someone is going to get around to figuring out where Bergstein is.'

'I know. If I can only get him to talk, I might be able to help him. But until I know who the killer is and can prove it, there's not much I can do.'

A pause, then she said quietly, 'Then I reckon you'd better do something fast, Johnny. If you have Donovan on your back again, it won't be long before he sniffs Bergstein out. Then there'll be hell to pay.'

The line went dead. I stood looking at the receiver, then replaced it in its cradle. She was right. She was always right. I had to think of something and I did the only thing I could think of.

I rang a number in New York. At least I had one friend there I could trust; a friend who had the necessary muscle to set things in motion.

The phone rang a number of times and then someone answered and I asked to speak to Ernie Whitehead. I'd known

Ernie for several years, ever since I'd come out of jail. As an FBI agent, he was one of the best and always on the level. Had it not been for him and Dawn, I'd probably have spent the rest of my life in and out of jail on some charge or other.

'Whitehead,' said the familiar voice.

'Johnny Merak,' I said.

'Johnny! Haven't heard from you for some time. What's on your mind?'

'A little problem here in LA. You probably heard that Carlos Galecci was murdered a little while back.'

'Sure. I picked up something about it. Knifed in the back in a locked vault. Nobody knows how it was done.'

'That's the one. I've been put on and off the case so many times I'm not sure where I am. But I've just picked up a material witness who could do with some protection, more than I can give him. I'm not certain whether he knows who the killer is but he knows enough to put the finger on someone.'

There was a pause as Whitehead thought that over. Then he said, 'I gather there's some reason why you haven't brought in LA Homicide on this?'

'The witness won't talk if I do that. Maybe he has some reason to believe there are some bent cops there and if he spills everything to them, he won't live long enough to testify at any trial that might come up.'

'I get the picture. Maybe it might help if I come down and take a look around myself. I've a case on at the moment but I can be there the day after tomorrow.'

'Thanks, Ernie. That'll be a great help. One other thing. Enrico Manzelli.'

'Manzelli! You reckon he's in on this?'

I could imagine his ears pricking up at the mention of Manzelli's name.

'No, he's definitely out on the sidelines. The fact is, I had a little chat with him a few days ago. He wants to nail Galecci's killer as much as I do. He practically ordered me to stay on the case.'

'You're playing in the big league this time, Johnny. Manzelli controls all of the mobs in LA. We'd like to pin something on him but so far he's stayed clean. You'd better watch your back where he's concerned.'

'It's not Manzelli I'm afraid of. There's a hood named Delano who's somehow hooked up with Galecci's widow. From what she's told me, she's planning to take control of Galecci's empire. Seems Carlos left it all to her in a will he made shortly before he was murdered.

'Sam Rizzio, Galecci's right-hand man, isn't going to take that lying down and it wouldn't surprise me if we have a full-scale gang war on the streets of LA before we know it. That could spell big trouble and I think it's what Manzelli is afraid of.'

There was a longer pause this time. I knew Whitehead was considering all of the possible ramifications of what I'd told him.

Then he said, 'Listen, Johnny. This is worse than I thought when you first came on. I'll get in touch right away with one of our agents in LA. His name is Clive Denton. I'll arrange for him to pick up this witness of yours and take him to a safe address where nobody will be able to get to him. Where is this witness now?'

I gave him Dawn's address.

'Right. Denton should be with you within a couple of hours. He's a tall guy, just over six-foot with a black moustache. He'll identify himself and take this witness off your hands. In the meantime, just sit tight. I'll be there myself the day after tomorrow.'

'Thanks, Ernie.' I put the phone down.

I turned to the brothers Bergstein. They sat silent on the settee, watching me, nothing showing on their faces. They could have been carved from stone for all the movement they made.

'It looks as though you're suddenly a very important witness,' I said, speaking to Simon. 'There'll be an FBI agent here within a couple of hours to take you to a place where you'll be safe.' I switched my gaze to Enunanuel. 'As for you, it might be better if you were to go with your brother. You're not the one these guys are after but if they figure you know anything, they'll wring it out of you somehow.'

I went to the cupboard, brought out a bottle of whiskey and poured three drinks.

'Here. You both look as though you

could do with this. I know I can.'

They accepted the drinks in silence.

I checked that both the doors were locked and then came back. The drink didn't taste as good as it usually did. Maybe I was too tensed, maybe I wasn't sure I was doing the right thing.

Ten minutes later there was the rattle of a key in the front door. Dawn came into the room.

She took off her coat. 'What's happening, Johnny?' Her voice was a little sharp as if she'd been rehearsing the question all the way from the office.

I told her and she listened in silence until I'd finished. Then she relaxed a little.

Nodding, she said, 'At last you're thinking with your head. If I'd known it was going to come to this, I'd have made you get in touch with Ernie right away. It could have saved a lot of trouble.'

'There was nothing to really go on at that time,' I reminded her. 'Nothing but hunches and they don't count for anything where the FBI is concerned.'

I looked across at Simon. He had

finished his drink. 'Do you feel like talking to me before this agent gets here? If you know who killed Galecci and Tefler you might as well — '

'Anton never told me the name of the killer, only how he suspected the murder might have been carried out. He possibly guessed who it was but he took that secret with him to the grave.'

I felt certain he was lying. But he wasn't going to talk. Not to me, anyway.

The next hour and a half dragged as though Father Time had a leash on the individual minutes. By now, that guy who had driven up to the cabin would have discovered he had been tricked and would be taking steps to rectify the mistake. If he was the killer, he would be feeling a little unsure of himself, knowing there was a witness around someplace who could testify against him. If he had been simply a paid hitman, he'd know his own life was on the line for allowing his quarry to slip so easily through his fingers.

After a couple more drinks I was beginning to feel like the tightrope walker in a circus. A thin line and a very big drop on either side. Things were happening out there, beyond the front door, and I had no idea what they were.

When the black limousine slid to a purring halt outside the front door there was nothing about it to mark it out from any of the others using the street. I stood with my shoulder against the wall and watched it from the window. The driver got out and stood beside it, one hand on the door, the other just inside his coat.

He might have appeared, to anyone watching, to be reaching for a pack of cigarettes. He kept turning his head to stare along the street in both directions. Then the passenger door opened and a second guy emerged. He stood well over six feet in his socks and sported a black moustache just as Whitehead had said.

Without a glance at his companion, he came up the path and knocked loudly on the door.

I went and opened it. He looked at me for a moment, then asked, 'Are you John Merak?'

I nodded.

His hand went to his inside pocket and

he pulled out a plastic card. It had his picture on it and identified him as Clive Denton, FBI. 'I understand you have a material witness here to be taken into protective custody.'

'That's right.' I opened the door wider and he stepped through. 'His name is Simon Bergstein. He knows something important about the Galecci killing but he won't talk to me.'

'I reckon he'll talk to us,' Denton said crisply. He walked over to where Bergstein sat on the settee. 'Mister Bergstein. I'm an FBI agent. You're to come with me. Do you understand?'

Bergstein eyed him blankly. Then he swallowed and gave a slight nod. 'I understand.'

'Good.' Denton glanced in Emmanuel's direction. 'I've no specific orders to take you but it might be better if you did come with us. If we consider it's safe for you to leave, you can at any time.'

'How long do I have to remain in custody?' Simon asked.

'That'll be up to my boss,' Denton told him. 'I don't make decisions like that. It will all depend upon what you have to tell us and whether the D.A. reckons he has a good case.'

Simon got to his feet. He swayed a little and strain made tramlines across his forehead. 'I'm ready,' he said in a whisper. 'I've had this thing on my mind too long. I'll be glad when it's all over.'

'Sure. I understand.' Denton ushered them to the door. Outside, the other agent was still eyeing the street up and down. He walked slowly around the car and opened the rear door. The two brothers got in and settled back. The driver eased himself behind the wheel. Denton raised a hand to me as they drove off.

I went back inside. I felt like another drink but decided against it.

Those little mice inside my brain were still running around, throwing up questions to which there seemed to be no answers.

Something was nagging at me but I couldn't dig it out and recognize it for what it was. It had something to do with Tefler's death but although I went over everything in my mind, nothing registered.

I decided there was nothing I could do until Whitehead arrived and I'd put him into the picture.

Dawn picked up the glasses from the table and took them into the kitchen.

I leaned back and closed my eyes. It had been one hell of a day. Surely things couldn't get any worse.

Ten minutes later, they began to get worse. There was a loud, insistent knocking on the door. I twisted in my seat to stare out of the window as Dawn walked through to answer it. I recognized the car a split second before I heard Donovan's voice.

'Is Merak here?'

'Yes. He's here.'

Dawn came in with Donovan behind her. He didn't sit down but stood just inside the doorway, his hat still jammed on the back of his head. He looked mad and pleased at the same time. There was a piece of paper in his hand and he thrust it towards Dawn.

'This is a warrant to search your

house,' he said tersely. 'I trust neither of you have any objections?' His tone implied that, if we had, he wasn't going to take any notice of them.

I looked across at Dawn and shrugged slightly. 'I don't know what you expect to find, Lieutenant,' I said, speaking as calmly as I could. 'But I guess you're welcome to look around.'

'Would you mind telling me what this is all about?' Dawn said. She glanced round quickly as the door opened again and two cops walked in.

Donovan gave them a brief nod and while one went upstairs, the other moved through into the kitchen. From the way they moved it was clear they were old hands at this kind of work. They'd miss nothing.

'Maybe if you were to tell us what you're looking for, Lieutenant, we could save you some time,' I said. 'After all, you must have something in mind. You wouldn't go to all the trouble to sweet-talk one of your judge friends into signing a warrant, just to mess the place up.'

Donovan turned his head and glared at me. His lips pulled back from his teeth like a dog about to savage its victim. 'You're too goddamn smart for your own good, Merak. But this time you've gone right over the line. I've had information passed to me from a reliable source that you're hiding a state witness in this house.'

I managed to look suitably surprised. 'That's against the law, isn't it, Lieutenant?'

The sarcasm wasn't lost on him. His scowl deepened. 'Don't play games with me. I happen to know you went to see the guy who has a shop next door to Anton Tefler.'

'Sure I went there,' I admitted. 'But I might just as well have saved myself the trip. The shop's closed up and there was no sign of him.'

'Only you weren't satisfied with that, were you? You questioned Mrs. Forsythe in the house opposite. And she told you what she told me. That he has a brother living at — '

'1266 East 24th Place,' I said. 'It's on

the other side of town.'

'I know damn well where it is.' Donovan's eyes lit up as if a flame had sparked behind them. 'So you don't deny you went to call on his brother?'

'Why should I deny it? It was the logical thing to do.'

'And he told you where Simon Bergstein was hiding out.'

I shook my head. 'No. He told me nothing. Claimed he hadn't spoken to his brother in years.'

The guy who'd been in the kitchen came in and shook his head mutely.

Donovan pointed into the back room and waited until the cop had gone.

'That's not the way I see it, Merak. Somehow, you found out that Simon Bergstein was holed up in one of those cabins out on top of the hill road. You went there which is why you weren't in your office when I phoned.'

'You're way out,' I said. 'If you knew Bergstein was there, why didn't you go out and pick him up?'

Donovan suddenly smiled as if I'd said something real funny. 'Odd that you should mention that. I did send one of my men up there. But the minute he got there a cab pulled away and headed back towards town. My man followed it but lost it in the traffic. I figure there were three men inside that cab. You, Bergstein and his brother. I also figure you brought them here, thinking it would be a safe place to hide them out until you could beat the truth out of one of them.'

'Does it look as though we've got them here, Lieutenant?' Dawn asked quietly.

The guy who had been upstairs came down, shaking his head. 'Nothing there, Lieutenant,' he said, almost apologetically. 'The place is clean.'

Donovan's smile froze as if caked in ice. His teeth were clamped so tightly inside his mouth I could almost hear them grinding together. Then he jerked a thumb towards the door. The two cops went out.

Donovan looked from Dawn to me. Then he said thinly, 'You've got him stashed away someplace, Merak. I'll wager my pension on that. But I'll find him, even if I have to take this whole city apart, street by street. And when I do, you'll be standing in the dock beside him.'

9

I was sitting behind the desk in the office, still trying to figure out things in my mind, a half empty cup of still-hot coffee in front of me, when Ernie Whitehead came in. He gave a quick look round the office, took in everything in that single glance, then gave Dawn a smile before pulling out the chair in front of the desk.

'It's good to see you again, Johnny,' he said genially. 'You too, Dawn. Pity that the only time we seem to get together is when there's big trouble.'

'That's the way of the world, Ernie,' I said, reaching forward and shaking hands. 'Would you like some coffee?'

'I'd appreciate it. I can't stand the stuff they pass off as coffee on these domestic flights.'

I knew Whitehead didn't drink, always said he couldn't stand the taste of it, so why waste money on something he didn't like and wake up with a hangover the next morning?

Dawn went over to the small electric kettle plugged into the wall socket and switched it on.

'Did everything go all right with this witness of yours?' he asked.

'No problem at all,' I said.

'Good. Now for the rest of it. What have you got so far?'

I went over everything from the call I'd got from Rizzio, which had been the start of the affair, to tracking Simon Bergstein to the cabin up in the hills. He listened attentively, not interrupting once.

'And you reckon it was the same person who killed both Galecci and this man Tefler?' he asked when I'd finished.

'I'm sure of it. Two identical knives, both men stabbed in the back. That seems to be the theme in this case.'

'And from what I gather, there are quite a number of people who wanted Galecci dead. The grieving widow — she stood to gain a lot and she evidently knew about the will. Maybe Rizzio. With Galecci out of the way he'd be kingpin in the mob. Either of them could also have murdered Tefler.'

'But we still haven't figured out how Galecci was killed,' Dawn put in.

'No, but from what you've told me, it has to be someone pretty smart. You think Rizzio or Mrs. Galecci could plan something like that?'

'Anything's possible.' I lit a cigarette.

Whitehead spread his hands. 'Maybe we can get something out of Bergstein. Obviously he knows something important.' He glanced at his watch. 'I'll go over there now. If he spills anything, I'll let you know.'

He picked up a piece of paper from the desk and scribbled a number on it.

'If you need to get hold of me in a hurry, ring that number.'

After he'd gone, I looked across at Dawn. She seemed more relaxed now. I guessed that Whitehead's presence made all the difference.

'What are you thinking about now, Johnny? You still worried somebody might get to Bergstein even with all the protection he's got?'

213

'It's not Bergstein that worries me,' said. 'It's something up here — '

I tapped the side of my head, ' — that won't go away. Something to do with the time we were in Tefler's shop.'

'Well, apart from his body, there was nothing there except those damned clocks and their infernal ticking.'

I jerked forward in my chair, staring at her. All of those little mice that had been running around inside my head had suddenly stopped.

Dawn must have noticed the change of expression on my face. 'What is it, Johnny?'

'That's the answer. That's how Galecci was killed. It's what Bergstein's been told. And if I'm right about one other thing, I know who the killer is.'

'Then if you're sure, don't you think you should let Whitehead know?'

I nodded. 'I'll ring him in a couple of minutes. First, I have to get in touch with Donovan. He has to be brought in on this as well.'

'Somehow, I don't think he'll thank you for solving his case for him.'

'You never know,' I said, reaching for the phone. 'I might get a medal for this.'

I dialed Donovan's number. The line burred a couple of times. Then he came on.

'Merak, Lieutenant,' I said. 'I've got some information I think may interest you.'

'Oh.' He didn't sound too interested. 'And what's that?'

'I've just figured out how Galecci was murdered in that vault. And I also reckon I know who killed him and Tefler.'

His tone changed at that. I could visualize him sitting at his desk, staring at the receiver and wondering whether I was having him on, or being deadly serious. He must have decided on the latter for he said in a cautious voice. 'All right, Merak. I'm listening.'

'Not over the phone,' I said. 'I wouldn't like to think there's a bug on this line, but it's possible.'

'Okay. Where? You want to come down to the precinct and tell me everything?'

I said nothing for a couple of minutes, giving him the impression I was thinking the suggestion over. 'I'll be there in half an hour,' I said finally.

'I'll be here and this had better be good.' There was a click as he put the phone down.

Dawn leaned forward over the desk and her smile had faded slightly. 'I hope you know what you're doing, Johnny.'

'I hope I'm finally earning that thousand dollar retainer Galecci gave me,' I said.

I put a call through on the number Whitehead had given me. He answered right away, almost as if he had been expecting it. I told him what I'd figured out and of the meeting I'd arranged with Donovan.

Then I went downstairs and out to where the Merc was parked. It still looked as battered as it had the day before. But it started right away and I made it through the traffic to the police precinct.

The desk sergeant looked bored. He finished dealing with some guy who'd been brought in on a suspected hold-up charge, then turned his attention to me.

He knew who I was but he still

persisted in asking my name. I told him and said I had an appointment with Lieutenant Donovan of Homicide.

'You know where his office is.' It was a statement and not a question. I nodded and he jerked his thumb towards the corridor.

Donovan's office was empty when I got there but a couple of minutes later he came striding briskly along the corridor with a sheaf of papers in one hand. He pushed open the door and motioned for me to go in. Sitting down behind the desk, he inclined his head towards the empty chair in front of him.

I sat down and waited while he scrawled his signature at the bottom of the pages. Then he pushed them to one side and looked up.

'All right, Merak,' he said coldly. 'You say you've figured out how Galecci was killed and who did it.'

'That's right.' There was an ashtray in front of me with a couple of cigarette butts in it. I took out a cigarette and lit it. 'Let me run it past you, Lieutenant. See what you make of it.'

'Go ahead. I'm listening.'

I blew some smoke and waved it away from the desk. 'What have we got? A locked vault and Galecci sitting at the table with a knife in his back. Nobody could have got in or out without him opening the door because he was the only one who knew the combination. The doc said he died some time around midnight. I say it was *exactly* midnight when he died.'

'You sure of that?' Donovan seemed interested.

'I'm damned sure.' I flicked some ash into the ashtray. He was watching every little movement I made, his eyes half closed.

'Go on.'

'There was nobody in the vault with him when he died. But the murder weapon was there, just waiting to be used.'

Donovan frowned. 'You realize you're not making any sense. If this is all you've got to tell me — '

'Oh, there's more. You see, my guess is that Galecci had a visitor that afternoon.

Maybe if I was to ask around, someone there could confirm that Galecci let his visitor in and took him down into the vault. When the killer left, everything was in place for the perfect murder.

'You see, that visitor brought Galecci a present. I noticed it at the time we found his body but it didn't click then. All those antique clocks worth maybe a million bucks in total — and one that was definitely not an antique sitting just behind the chair where Galecci sat every night, going through the accounts for the day.'

'Not an antique?' Donovan's voice was now icily cold.

'That's right. Oh, it was a beautiful piece of art and made by a master craftsman — Anton Tefler. I've no doubt he made it to order. A cuckoo clock that would have graced any collection. Only this one was very special. My guess is that it chimed only twice every day, dead on the strokes of twelve. But there was no cuckoo popping out at midnight. There was only a knife, propelled by a powerful spring, powerful enough to pierce Galecci to the heart.'

'Then if you've figured out that much, who's the killer?'

'That took a bit more figuring out. It could have been any number of people who all wanted Galecci dead. But then Tefler had to be killed. And a nosy dick and his assistant just happened to be on the premises just after it happened. I saw the knife that was used to kill Tefler. If you remember, I remarked at the time that it was an identical twin to that which had killed Galecci. I figured then that there were two identical knives and it was that which threw me at the time.'

'You're saying there weren't?'

'No. There was only one. The knife that was in Tefler's back was the same one that killed Galecci. Once I realized this, I asked myself: Who could possibly have got hold of that knife after Galecci was killed without being suspected?'

'And you came up with some answer?'

'I came up with the only answer. Only one person could have got hold of that knife after Galecci was killed. The one person who took it away as police evidence.'

Nothing changed in Donovan's face. He moved his right hand slightly, tapping gently with his fingers on the desk top.

'You think you're smart, don't you, Merak? Accusing me of murder. None of this will stand up in court. You realize that? Just some fantastic story concocted by a dick who has to maintain his reputation. What proof is there that there weren't two different knives? What proof is there that this clock you talk about ever existed?'

'Proof,' I said, 'is always something a murderer tries to get rid of. I've no doubt you had the run of that vault after Galecci was killed. Maybe that clock is no longer there. Maybe it, too, was removed as police evidence. Maybe it no longer exists.'

'Maybe it never did exist, except in your imagination.'

'True. But there's always Simon Bergstein. It wasn't one of your men who went up to that cabin to bring him in as a material witness. It was you and he wasn't supposed to be brought in for protective custody. He was to be shot while resisting a law officer.'

Donovan's face suddenly turned a bright shade of crimson. I thought he was going to have a stroke. Finally, he snapped, 'More fancy theorizing on your part, Merak.'

His right hand moved away from the desk top. He opened a drawer and put his hand in. When it came out, it was holding a gun. A gun that was pointed in my direction.

'I think you've just said a little too much.' His voice was like a rasp grating across metal.

'So you think you can shoot me here — in your office. That would take a lot of explaining to the D.A. And you can't claim self-defense because I'm not carrying my gun.'

He shook his head. 'That never entered my mind,' he said softly. 'You and me are going for a little drive. Nobody here is going to ask any questions when we walk out of here.'

'And I'll just disappear. But I can't see

how you'll stop Bergstein from talking. Tefler spilt the lot to him. I'm willing to bet it was exactly as I've just told you.'

He stood up. 'On your feet. Don't give me any trouble. And as for Bergstein. He doesn't worry me too much. I've got six men out looking for him right now. It's only a matter of time before we run him down.'

'I'll save you the trouble,' I said, getting to my feet. 'I know exactly where he is.'

His eyes widened at that. 'Where?'

'He's in protective custody with the FBI. If you want to know any more, you can ask the guy who's been standing behind you in the doorway all the time we've been talking.'

Donovan's head turned sharply. Ernie Whitehead came into the office. There were a couple of other men at his back and they both carried rifles.

'You'd better put that gun down, Donovan.' Whitehead said. 'I'm taking you in for murder.'

Donovan's eyes were a dull gray like dirty water. For a moment, I thought he intended to use the gun and to hell with the consequences. Then he placed it carefully on the desk.

'Did you get all of that, Ernie?' I asked.

'I heard enough,' Whitehead said. He motioned to the two agents who walked into the office and took up positions on either side of Donovan. They led him outside.

'Bergstein okay?'

'Sure. He's fine. He's admitted that Tefler told him just how that murder had been committed. Seems Donovan had something on Tefler that went back many years. Something about immigration irregularities. We could have nailed Donovan without you risking your neck like that.'

'Let's just say it was a boost to my professional ego. I owed it to Galecci.'

Whitehead snorted derisively. 'One of these days that professional ego is going to be the finish of you.'

I changed the subject. 'Donovan must have really hated Galecci to bide his time for five years before killing him. It wouldn't be too difficult to get in to plant that clock. He'd probably tell Galecci it was a peace offering, a gift to let bygones be bygones. Had it not been for having to get rid of Tefler, he would have got away with the perfect murder.'

'Well, that's another case closed.' Whitehead accompanied me to the door.

We went down the stairs together and out into the hazy sunlight of the car park.

'I've just one more phone call to make,' I said as we shook hands. 'Much as I dislike doing it, I have to let Manzelli know — if he doesn't know already. He did tell me to stay with the case.'

Whitehead grinned. 'I didn't hear any of that,' he said.

★ ★ ★

The evening papers carried the news of Donovan's arrest with banner headlines on the front page. There was another item on an inside page which wasn't given such prominence. Both Delano and Gloria Galecci had been killed outright when the car they were traveling in had failed to take a steep bend some twenty miles outside of town. The driver, who had recently arrived from Chicago, was also killed. According to the report, a preliminary examination of the car had revealed there was scarcely any brake fluid in the brake pipes.

I rang Rizzio and got through first time. I gave him the news about Donovan.

'So that's how it was done,' he said. 'A pity Gloria isn't around to hear it. I told her several times to have those brakes checked. But like Carlos she was too stubborn to take any advice.'

'Sure,' I agreed. 'She was like that.'

I put the phone down. Gloria, Delano and that hood from Chicago all gone in one instant of tangled wreckage. I thought for a minute about Galecci, sitting there in his locked vault, checking the records as he did every night, in the one place where he was safe from any danger.

Until midnight — not knowing that that was the perfect time for murder!